EVEN HEROES CRY

Fords of Nashville Series

USA Today Bestselling Author
HILDIE McQUEEN

Pink Door Publishing

Copyright Hildie McQueen 2024
Print Edition

All rights reserved. No part of this book may be reproduced in any form or by any electronic or mechanical means—except in the case of brief quotations embodied in critical articles or reviews—without written permission.

Thank you for respecting the hard work of this author.

The characters and events portrayed in this book are fictitious. Any similarity to real persons, living or dead, is purely coincidental and not intended by the author.

Also by Hildie McQueen
(In reading order)

Fords of Nashville
Even Heroes Cry
The Last Hero
Nobody's Hero

Laurel Creek Trilogy
Jaded: Luke
Broken: Taylor
Ruined: Tobias

Other Works
Montana Bachelor
Montana Beau
Montana Boss
Montana Bred
Montana Born
Melody of Secrets
Cowboy in Paradise

Dedication

This book is dedicated to all the service men and women who fought and are still fighting over in Iraq and Afghanistan. May you find a reason to move on when you come home. God bless you and keep you safe.

Chapter One

IN SPITE OF its sagging porch and missing column, the used-to-be-white, three-story Victorian at the end of a curving tree-lined street stood proud. With its peeling paint and lopsided shutters, which were missing more slats than not, the house would be her best friend, the shoulder to cry on and the healing solace for Tesha Washington's shattered soul.

"It's definitely a fixer-upper." Her companion, Cleve, leaned back on the side of his new silver Camaro and shielded his eyes with his hand. "I don't know what in the hell you're thinking, Tesh. It's too much work."

Tesha stood in front of the house and faced him, her arms held wide until getting his full attention. "Look at me and then to the house. Really look at it. When I look in the mirror that is what I see. A barely held together exterior and a total wreck on the inside."

Somehow Tesha had to get it through his hard head this was exactly where she had to be. "Please understand how much I need this house, Cleve. This is where I belong right now."

Lovely, Tennessee. A town she'd found when searching for foreclosed Victorian houses. She'd never heard of it, but once she researched it on the internet, it called to her. She'd driven nonstop from Atlanta and upon seeing the town, had instantly fallen in love with the sweeping hills, old stately trees, and small friendly downtown area. Now if she could get Cleve to comprehend.

The sadness in Cleve's eyes almost stopped her from trying to get him to understand. There was no way in hell her friend was going to leave her there alone if he thought she'd finally lost her ever-loving mind.

Cleve had once been her boyfriend, but after a few months of awkward attempts at being lovers, they'd respected each other enough to realize they were better suited for friendship. Tall, dark, and handsome, Cleve wore jeans and a dress shirt that she knew cost a pretty penny. Tesha always thought Cleve could walk onto any magazine shoot and fit right in.

His coffee-colored skin glistened under the sun when he rolled the sleeves of the pale green shirt up his forearms. "I worry that you're in over your head. That you'll sink your money into this…" He stepped around her and kicked at a hole in one of the front stairs. His tan Gucci loafer broke through the rotting wood. "See that. It's a money pit, Tesh."

She winced at the scratches on the expensive shoe. The hole in the stair was an easy fix. Once the interior was completed to her liking, she'd tackle the outside. A tingle of excitement at getting started sent a shiver through her.

"I love this house already." She reached for his hand and held it up to her face. Her lips curved when he let out a conceding sigh. Yet, his dark eyes remained hard under the angry slashes of his brows. "I'm going to have to drive to this, what barely passes for a town, regularly just to check on you."

Once again she studied the front façade of the once extravagant entryway. "The house and I have many things in common. With every stroke of a brush and every pound of a hammer, I will bring her back and one day she will be perfect." She met his gaze with intent. "And I will be closer to being whole again. I can just feel it."

She gave him a wide smile. "Don't you believe in my abilities as a designer?"

"I do." He shoved his hands into his pockets and looked to the surrounding homes. "Nice houses on this street. Too country for my tastes, but the architecture here is beautiful. I wouldn't be surprised if all your new neighbors bring pies and cookies over before the end of the week."

"The real estate agent gave me the low down on some of the neighbors." Tesha pointed to the house on the right side of her property line. A proud brick house with four tall columns sat away from the street behind a high black iron fencing with elaborate gates. "The Walkers are an old southern family. The couple who lives there now are in their fifties and very active in the town council." Tesha peered toward the home's front lawn. "Looks like they own a small horse."

Cleve went to the fence then began to laugh. "It's a Great Dane. God, Tesh, you're definitely not ready for country life if you think that dog is a horse."

Tesha rolled her eyes and swept her hand to the house on the other side of her property. A red Queen Anne style home sat in pristine condition. A three-story hexagonal tower stood out on the front façade echoed by a rounded porch on the opposite side. It was an inspiration to what she would achieve. "A war veteran lives there. The agent said he rarely ventures to out. He leaves only to go to the grocery or the hardware store."

"An old guy?"

Tesha nodded. "That's the impression I get."

The Walker's automatic iron gates opened and a large blue GMC truck pulled through. The woman in the passenger seat rolled down her window and waved. "Welcome, new neighbors." A blond woman with perfect make up and a bright pink tank top smiled at them. "I'm Jo-Lynn Walker. I'll be by later this week to introduce myself properly." A man she assumed was her husband gave them a nod from the driver's side.

"Hello, I'm Tesha." Tesha smiled brightly, happy to make her first acquaintance. "This is my friend, Cleve."

Tesha placed her hands on her hips and watched the truck disappear. "I think small town living will grow on me."

"We agree on that. This is definitely a small town. Not one single Starbucks." Cleve shook his head. "I don't think I'd like it here."

"You're a spoiled snob, Cleve." Tesha slipped her arm around his and leaned into him. "Look at the surroundings. Really look. The richness of the landscape, the quaint buildings and huge horse farms nearby are beautiful. It's the cozy feeling I get in my chest when I take it all in that made me decide this is where I should live right now."

Finally his eyes softened and he pulled her closer against his side. They stood hip-to-hip for several minutes. "All right. I'm still going to worry about you a bit. But I understand. You need to do something. Staying in Atlanta surrounded by all the familiar things and the memories made it too hard to move on."

"I couldn't stay there any longer. David's parents are put out with me. They think I'm crazy for renting out our home and moving. But after two long years of trying to get past his death, and continue with my life without success, something had to give. They're not speaking to me now. That's not fair."

"They'll come around."

"Maybe. I sent them a couple boxes of his things with a note to keep it for me until I'm settled in. I wonder if I'll ever get any of it back." Sadness crept into the edges of her smile and Tesha blinked away the mistiness in her eyes. "They are hurting, and I can understand that. Everyone grieves differently. In a way, I am a reminder of their son and it's probably for the best that I put space between us."

"Take your time, make the most out of this, but don't let pride keep you here if you need to come home to Atlanta." Cleve kissed her forehead. "If you change your mind at any time, call me. I'll be here within hours and help you pack up."

"What if I decide to stay?" She smiled up at him. "What will you do then?"

Cleve lifted and lowered his shoulders. "Then I suppose I'll be coming to Tennessee on a regular basis. Maybe even open a Starbucks."

"Don't do that." Tesha moved away from him and pointed to the U-Haul she'd driven. "Come on, let's unhitch my vehicle and unload. I'll treat you to dinner in town. I hear the diner has a great pot pie."

"Seriously? Can you please not make me eat that?" Cleve groaned in mock angst. "I have to drive back and don't want to burp the entire way."

"Stop picking on my new town." Tesha laughed and punched his shoulder.

She scanned the front of the home and visualized it pristine and open to friends and family. "Do you still agree with my idea of opening a Bed and Breakfast away from the hustle and bustle of a large city? It will be a place of relaxation and renovation. I've considering weekends exclusively for war widows and give them a place to get away and spend time alone. It's what I feel I need to do right now."

Cleve kissed her temple. "I know, Tesh. I just hope it's what you should be doing and it does help you heal."

TESHA CLIMBED THE wide stairs to the red front door of the veteran's house. She let out a breath, swept the long bangs of her pixie cut hair behind her ear and pressed the doorbell button.

Like the rest of the house, it was framed with an ornate wooden cutout painted ash green to match the trim on the windows and doors. The low dongs of the chime sounded and she resisted the urge to cup her hands around her eyes and peek in one of the glass panes.

After a few moments without an answer, she placed her finger on the doorbell, contemplating if she should press it again. She'd caught sight of her reclusive neighbor's large black truck as it drove past her house to the back of his drive a couple hours earlier, so she knew he was home.

Perhaps he was not just a loner, but didn't care for company and would not open the door. If after the second ring the door didn't open, she'd write him a note and leave it somewhere he'd find it.

But where? She studied the door and wall beside it. There was no mail slot. The mailbox was on the street, and it was illegal to place anything inside it. She pressed the button and once again the two-toned ring echoed inside the house.

If the man was in the bathroom or otherwise occupied, it was best for her to return and figure out where to leave a note. It was disappointing. She really wanted to start plotting her garden. It might be silly to focus on gardening with all the work that needed to be done inside, but it was a priority. Especially now before the weather became too unbearable to spend hours outdoors. It was already late spring and the days were becoming hotter. One of the reasons she'd purchased the property was the large area to the left side between their homes.

Her hands in the dirt always gave her a sense of purpose. She'd only begun gardening a few months before leaving Atlanta and her garden there had thrived. Now she looked forward to it again. A place of beauty to rest and read, spend hours maintaining it and being responsible for beauty and fragrance. It would not only be her solace but also force her to spend time outdoors. Once the garden was finished and flourishing, from both her living room and kitchen windows, she'd be able to look out and enjoy it all year long. The only thing stopping her from sketching a complete diagram was she didn't know exactly where the property line was.

She'd looked at the plat drawings her realtor had given her, but when she walked the area she'd had a hard time figuring it out. Besides, she'd rather not plant trees or shrubbery without at least speaking to the guy next door to make sure he would not have an issue with it.

Standing in the shaded area, Tesha felt the cool breeze that caused the one fern hanging on a hook, to sway between arches. The front porch was pristine, as was the rest of the house. The only thing missing was a nice set of wicker chairs and some additional greenery to make the space inviting.

She studied the shutters that flanked the large front window. They looked to be newly made, but at the same time the cut of the wood and the paint fit the Victorian perfectly. Since no one answered, she took the liberty of inspecting the workmanship on the porch railing. Amazing how well he matched the shape of the new posts to the old. Whoever did the work was definitely an expert woodcrafter. Tesha looked to the door with a frown. If only he'd open it. Along with her first issue of finding out the parameters of her property, now she needed to know who did the woodwork. She'd love to get the same person to do some work at her house.

Just as she pressed her finger onto the doorbell one last time, the door opened and Tesha lost her breath. Her sharp inhale the only sound for a few seconds.

In the doorway stood the most stunning man she'd ever laid eyes on. Never again would she roll her eyes at the mention of the word "breathtaking." His penetrating blue gaze took her in. Didn't just look at her eyes, but dove into them.

He stood about six foot three, but it was not his height alone that made him impressive. It was the massive expanse of his shoulders, the broad muscular chest, thick-corded neck and square jawline. It took a moment to realize they both stood staring at one another without speaking.

He didn't seem discomfited at her silence, but stood like a statue. If not for the barely noticeable lifting and lowering of his chest she'd think him not real. Long lashed grey blue eyes met hers. They darkened to a deeper blue and his nostrils flared just enough to let her know he was affected by her presence. Whether in a good way or bad way, she had no idea.

Tesha flushed under the intense scrutiny, and the raw attraction she felt instantly. The haze in her mind somewhat lifted and she held her right hand out to him. "Hello. I'm Tesha Washington. Your new neighbor."

The eyes moved slowly from her face down to her chest and finally to her outstretched hand. His much larger hand swallowed hers.

"Adam Ford." At the touch, her lips parted, but she recovered enough not to gasp again like a Jane Austen character, and shake his hand. When he did not release it, she pulled free of his loose grip.

Unable to speak, she stood frozen, her brain failing to engage and remember what she'd come over for. Maybe later it would seem odd that she'd not felt any compulsion to escape, to put distance between them like she'd done with every man who looked at her with even remote interest. Since David's death, any man's attention caused her guilt or awkward discomfort. It could her discomfort with men after David was the main reason things didn't work out with Cleve.

But not this man. He made her want to move closer to touch him.

A wonderful aroma of oregano, tomato, and garlic tickled her nose and Tesha sniffed the air. "Something smells amazing."

Adam looked over his shoulder into the house. It was then she noticed a kitchen towel draped across it. "I'm cooking." His eyes slanted to the floor and then up to her. Surely it was not meant as flirtation, but the sweep of his lashes made her stomach flip. *He cooked?* His throat moved when he swallowed and cleared it. Each one of the handsome man's movements sensual, without meaning to be. Tesha could barely drag her eyes from his throat to meet his gaze. "I'm sorry I didn't mean to interrupt whatever you're doing. I can come back another time."

Once again he remained silent, his face stoic except for what she translated as interest when his gaze roamed from her eyes to her lips. He took an awkward step back. "Please, come in."

When he turned to walk, her eyes popped wide at his perfectly formed behind. Now that was what she called booty. Her mouth practically watered wondering what it would feel like to have that taut area of his body under her palms. He wore loose sweatpants that hung low on his narrow hips, the worn fabric leaving very little to the imagination. When her mind went there, Tesha secretly thanked God he could not see her reaction to his tush. Ashamed at her thoughts, she rubbed a hand over her cheeks and dragged her eyes away to take in the interior of the house.

And…that was all it was, an interior. Not one stick of furniture in the entryway, the living room also completely empty, the gleaming hardwood floors bare of any rugs. The walls were equally as undecorated without any type of pictures, portraits, or even drapes around the windows. Two round columns separated the living room and what could possibly be a dining area. Hard to tell since, like the other rooms, it was bare of any articles. The columns were carved with an intricate ivy pattern that swirled from the floor to the top. Tesha stopped to admire them. "Beautiful."

"Thank you." Adam stood behind her, close enough Tesha swore his body heat warmed her back. She didn't dare turn around. "The woodworking in your home has to be the best I've ever seen."

"The craftsman is from Nashville, a friend of the folks. He does great work."

"I doubt I could afford him."

"He's a nice guy, would probably work around your budget." Adam walked around her to the center of a large kitchen, thankfully hidden from the waist down by a tall counter or she would have had a hard time keeping her eyes from wandering.

Sandstone countertops took her attention next. The appliances were all hidden behind the cherry wood cabinetry. An enormous farm style sink with a gooseneck faucet had room for any size pot. Unlike the rest of what she'd seen, the kitchen was fully furnished with four barstools in front of a high counter as well as an oval, matching cherry wood dining table and six chairs.

Adam motioned to a barstool opposite of the counter. "Please sit. I'll get this stuff out of the oven. It'll only take a moment."

Although he spoke politely, she couldn't call him friendly. He'd yet to smile, his expression more stoic than anything. His southern manners came into play when she sat. His deep voice held a slight southern accent. "I apologize for not coming to introduce myself when you moved in a few days ago." He glanced to the oven and took the kitchen towel from his shoulder.

Tesha smiled at his attempt to make casual conversation. "It's fine. In Atlanta no one introduces themselves, so I didn't even think about it. This is all new to me." She watched him open the oven door and pull out a casserole dish then place it on the counter. Afterwards, he took out a second one and did the same. "Lasagna?"

Adam nodded, eyes on the dishes. "Yes. My mother's birthday gift. Mom insisted she wanted my lasagna." He threw the towel back over his shoulder in what she pegged to be a habit and opened the refrigerator.

While he disappeared behind the door, she stood and walked closer to the food. Not just to get another whiff, but it gave her a better view of his backside. "Does your mother live near here?"

He straightened with two soft drinks and held one out to her after popping the top. "About an hour and a half away, in the outskirts of Nashville."

Wearing a tank top with what looked to be a tomato stain on the front, she was able to admire his bulging biceps. He replied to her questions but did not ask or elaborate. Tesha drank the sweet liquid and realized he was being polite but not inviting the conversation to continue.

Suddenly she felt awkward. She'd overstayed her welcome and needed to get to the reason for her visit. "I…" His eyes immediately locked to hers and her throat went dry. She took another sip of her drink. "I came to talk to you about my plans for a gated garden on this side of the house." Tesha motioned toward her house. "Do you have time to walk around with me so I can tell you what I have in mind and make sure you don't have a problem with it?"

"I can't right now."

"Oh. Of course, I don't expect you to do it right now. I can wait until a better day." Actually she did hope he'd to walk outside with her, she wanted to start on the garden. But maybe he had plans she'd interrupted with her impromptu visit.

"I'll come over, maybe later today." Although he looked at her as if he was a starving man and she the last ham sandwich on the planet, he did not move, instead remained frozen behind the kitchen island, his untouched drink in front of him.

It was time to leave. Tesha wondered how she could make a graceful exit. She couldn't figure out if he was bothered by her visit and wished her gone or if perhaps this would be a good opportunity to invite him over for a meal and maybe get to know him better. She did a quick scan of the surrounding spaces. No woman's touch anywhere. He was definitely not in a relationship.

Chapter Two

FOR THE FIRST time since returning to Tennessee, two years earlier, Adam was glad to have moved into the huge, empty Victorian.

Other than the recently renovated kitchen where he spent a great deal of time, the house served as a constant reminder of things best left forgotten.

She stood just a few feet away, separated by the kitchen counter. The new and astonishingly gorgeous next-door neighbor. Thank God for kitchen counters, the obstacle kept him from moving closer and making a total fool of himself.

Every time Tesha Washington spoke, the musical sound soothed his mind. He could listen to her talk all day. Her voice had a slight southern lilt, while at the same time she spoke with the fast precision brought on from living in the city.

But it wasn't her voice that shook him upon opening the front door. It was seeing how stunning she was up close. The small woman struck him as the perfect mixture of innocence and sexiness. Somehow she managed equal measures of elegance, grace, and down-to-Earth easiness. Dressed casually, she made a pair of tight jeans and simple soft pink t-shirt mind-blowingly sexy. Her fingers caressed the soft drink bottle, her short nails painted in soft pink. His attention on her hands, he wondered what those fingernails would feel like digging into his back.

Adam cleared his throat and considered what to say to keep her just a bit longer. It was moments like this he hated his shy nature. Although long silences didn't bother him in the least, it made others uncomfortable.

She was an exception to the stretches of silence. Instead of seeming discomfited, she took the time to look around and take in the kitchen details. Her eyes flitting here and there, landing on him on occasion, before moving to take in something else. He could see the wheels turning in her head, taking notes for her upcoming projects. When she bit her lip and cocked her head to look at the side of the counter, he held on to the one in front of him to keep from lunging toward her and tasting the very morsel her white perfect teeth teased.

Days earlier, he'd spied her from his second story window. The day she and her man moved in. The couple stood facing the front of the neglected house, his arm around her shoulders with the familiarity of two people who've known each other for a long time. While her companion looked on not seeming at all happy, the expression on her face was something he'd never forget.

Completely enthralled, with a wide smile, she'd stared at the old white house in awe. But it was her eyes that mesmerized him. They were filled with pure raw adoration, seeing the possibilities in beauty hidden by years of weathering and abandonment.

What he wouldn't give for someone to look at him like that one day. He'd seen the look of pure affection before, when his parents looked at each other. If ever anyone had any doubt true love existed, they were proof it did.

Once he'd thought to have found it with his ex-wife. But he soon discovered she adored his money and social position he provided more than him.

Tesha ran her hand over the counter top and down the side. "This sandstone works perfectly with the other details in the kitchen. I would have not considered it. I love how it brings out the tans and browns in the wood flooring and cabinetry."

"I think so too."

Where was her husband? The man left the next morning and he'd not seen the sporty silver Camaro since. What fool would leave a beauty like her alone for so many days? Someone very secure in his relationship he supposed.

Each time her gaze swept over him, his body hummed with awareness he long thought dormant. Adam did his best to control any reaction she caused from showing. It was unfortunate the day she came over all he'd done was pull on a worn set of sweatpants over his bare ass. He moved to stand closer behind the kitchen island, the second barrier helped. But not much.

No way was he walking outside with her right now to look at property lines and such. The thin material of his pants did not come close to hiding very much.

She lifted her hand and ran her fingers through her short-cropped hair. Tesha's thick black hair was styled in a short modern cut with a long sweep of bang that she hooked behind her right ear. She was petite, about five-four he guessed, with delicate bone structure. Her brown eyes were slanted on the outside corners, a very striking feature. Her lips were pouty and naturally curved up, making her look as if she were keeping an adorable secret.

She sipped from her bottle, her eyes on the casserole dishes he'd just pulled from the oven. The lasagna his mother insisted he bring over for her birthday. It was obviously an excuse for him to visit.

Miriam Ford's attempts at getting him to the family gathering were obvious. At the same time it assured him that his parents never stopped loving him and tried as best they could to understand what he went through.

He'd already planned to attend his mother's birthday celebration, the one day every year he made sure to show up at his parents' home. It had been too long since he'd seen his brothers together. Maybe it would keep them from dropping by as often, as they tended to do on occasion. Each of his brothers visited with a range of excuses, the same shadows of worry, they tried without success to hide in their expressions.

He loved his family more than anything, but it was exhausting to keep the demons hidden from them. When he returned from spending the day with his family it could turn into a hard night. But it was worth it.

His guest put her bottle on the counter and stood. "I better get out of your way. When you have a chance, just knock on the door and we can walk around the area where I'm planning to set up the garden. I'll show you what I have in mind and make sure you are okay with the part that will face your house." She smiled and let out a breath and Adam fought to keep from gawking at her breasts.

She continued. "I will make sure it's attractive from both sides of the fencing."

Tesha placed both hands on the counter, the specks of its

color almost matching her bronzed skin perfectly. He'd think of her alluring skin each time he'd look at the counter now. How soft it must be to his touch. Soft and supple under his lips.

Adam realized she was waiting for a reply. "I'll come over." He motioned for her to walk ahead of him to the door. He had two good reasons for it, a good view of her curves and not having to worry about her catching his body's reactions to her tantalizing scent, a mixture of vanilla and lavender. He followed and inhaled all the while his eyes roaming from her proud shoulders to the enticing curves of a small waist and round little bottom.

Tesha stopped and waited by the door. It was obvious she'd been raised in a home where manners and etiquette were followed. He pulled the door ajar, moving to stand partially behind it. Tesha lifted her face to look at him. "See you soon, neighbor." Her lips grabbed his attention. He could swear she purposefully taunted him, somehow knowing he found her irresistible.

"Nice to meet you, Tesha Washington."

He watched her prance down the stairs and cut through his side yard toward hers. Suddenly his yard took on a magical appeal. Adam walked outside to stand on the porch and stared at her retreating form until she disappeared into her house.

His cell phone jingled. Without looking he knew it was his mother calling to make sure he was coming this weekend. She'd not relax until he reassured her. He glanced once more toward the neighboring house. It was best if he went to visit Tesha that day. After visiting with his large family, he'd need a few days alone just in case.

ADAM TOOK THE same shortcut Tesha had earlier to her house a couple hours later. Since the renovation was completed, it was rare that he spent any time in the yard other than to mow grass and trim hedges. He'd dedicated all his time to repairing the interior of house. It took him an entire year to renovate the inside. He'd hired a carpenter from Nashville to complete the needed repairs and then spent the last nine months on the exterior, replaced what needed to be, stripped and painted every inch.

Once he stepped over the property line, it was obvious no one had taken care of the lawn. Although it had been recently cut, more weeds than grass covered the ground. He'd caught sight of men with lawn equipment making quick work of trimming and mowing. Tesha must have hired a lawn service to give the land some semblance of control of the overgrown greenery. When he reached the side door, he wondered if perhaps it was best to round the house and go to the front.

Before he moved, the side door opened and Tesha greeted him with a bright smile. "Hi. I'm so glad you came now." Instead of inviting him in, she climbed down the two wide stairs of the small side deck.

"I have to be honest, I am anxious to start this project. Now I can plan a trip to the nursery tomorrow or the next day." She grinned and he swallowed looking toward the ground to keep from staring at how stunning she looked in the shadows from the setting sun. "I've only recently began gardening, so I can't wait to start one here. I have a feeling it will flourish."

Her smile dimmed and she turned away. "I'm sorry. I know I'm babbling. It's crazy not having anyone to talk to for days. I don't mean to go on and on."

It was his fault that she'd stopped smiling, so he tried to come up with something to say. "I like hearing you talk. Your excitement is nice." Adam dug his hands into his pockets and waited.

"Oh." Once again, she gifted him with a wide smile. "Don't tell me that. I'll talk your ear off." Her laughter was light and airy. "Now, picture this. Stand here." Tesha instructed taking his arm and pulling him to the side of the stairs. Her hand was soft and the warmth of her touch was too brief.

"All right." She faced him and gestured to her right with a sweep of her arm. "I am thinking to have a short four-foot brick wall built from the edge of the front of the house to here." She shimmied backward and held her arms out. "Across here with an arbor over here." He couldn't help being mesmerized by her hurried moves as she rushed to stand to the opposite side of her imaginary front wall. "The other wall will be here almost to the side of the house. I will have a gate on this end." She exhaled. "Hope to find an old wrought iron gate to recycle."

He nodded and pictured what she planned to do. It sounded like she had it all calculated. Adam didn't understand why she needed to talk to him about it. Not that he minded it one bit. "You have it all planned out. Why do you need walls?"

Shadows crossed her face. Her eyes fell to her feet as she deliberated how much to share. He knew the look, had seen it many times in the faces of soldiers he'd served with. The tug of war between trust and only sharing enough to allow a point to come across. "I need a space for quiet time. Outside with fresh air, but at the same a feeling of privacy."

When he nodded in understanding, once again Tesha became animated. "I will plant English ivy that will eventually cover the bricks and the arbor. Also there will be some shrubbery on the outside to keep it from looking too obvious. I don't want to ruin any view you may have from your house."

Ah, so she was taking him into consideration. Ensuring her plans did not bother her neighbor. Tesha Washington was not only a beautiful woman, but caring and thoughtful too. She stood waiting for him to say something, and Adam considered that if he agreed too fast, their time together would end and he'd not have an excuse to spend time with her again. "Who is building the wall?" He kept a stern look, his brows drawn together. "What color brick."

She hurried back to the stairs and picked up a brick he'd not noticed. "I found these behind the house in a pile. The rest will come from this fireplace that will be demolished." He stalked after her when she rushed to stand by a partial brick fireplace. "I'm having it removed. This sidewall will be all windows." Tesha made swiping motions with her arms at the side of the house. He found it adorable.

He'd run out of questions. As was his habit, he shoved his hands into the front pockets of the worn jeans again and pretended to ponder what she'd explained. Tesha touched his arm and he looked to her. "The garden will come to here." She pulled on his arm again and walked alongside until they stood beside each other a few feet away, facing his house. "I am pretty sure it's safely within my property line."

A new excuse to see her again struck. "Yes, it's nowhere close to mine. I'll check to make sure but I may have some bricks in the shed out back. I can bring them over when you're ready to start. I have no problem with anything you're planning." Although he'd hate to lose the chance to catch glimpses of her while she worked on her garden. Then again, he would be able to from his second floor bedroom window.

"Thank you so much." Tesha beamed and threw her arms around his middle giving him a quick half hug. Hell he'd tear down a wall with his bare hands to bring her the bricks now.

She released him, not seeming to notice how intimate her touch had been. "From the porch of your house you should be able to see the garden. I'm hoping it will give you a nice view too."

Lightning flashed overhead. A summer storm would bring rain in a few minutes. A different set of lights flashed in his mind and Adam knew he had to get away from Tesha. "I have to make a phone call. Have a good night." Not even giving her time to respond, he rushed home. Before he made it to his door thunder clapped and boomed above. His breathing was harsh. Instead of his house, he saw entirely different surroundings.

Adam fumbled with the doorknob and managed to stumble indoors before falling to the floor.

Within minutes panic seized and he lost control. Flashes and thunder roared and he began to lose the battle against reality.

His face wet with perspiration, Adam dragged his convulsing body to the closest corner and rolled into a ball to wait for the panic to subside. Although it never helped, he covered his ears with his hands to wait for what could be hours or sometimes even days. It couldn't be days. He prayed for it to be over soon so he could make it to his parents'.

Chapter Three

THE FIRST VIEW of the contractor's truck coming to her house should have brightened her morning, but instead she groaned and rushed to the bathroom to splash water onto her face. Tesha doubted she got three hours of sleep the night before.

Atlanta summer storms rarely lasted as long as the one last night in Lovely. The rain raged on for hours. The booms of thunder shook the house and frightened her awake several times. She'd managed to fall asleep after it stopped sometime in the early morning hours, only to wake up gasping for air from a nightmare. Any memory of her dream was gone, but she supposed it must have been terrible by the way she'd been trembling.

Outside, a loud pop followed an unnatural screech when the ancient truck pulled to a stop on the driveway. On the truck's driver side door the words "Shanty and Sons" was spray-painted in crooked red letters. Moments later, knocks on the door echoed through her mostly empty house. Finally the start of the largest project would begin. She couldn't wait to tear down dilapidated walls and replace them with fresh drywall.

A burly bearded middle-aged man greeted her by removing his paint splatter stained hat. "Miss Washington, I'm Fred

Shanty, from Shanty and Sons." Next to him stood a slim man who couldn't possibly be his son, by the grey whiskers and lined face. Mr. Shanty pointed to his companion. "This here is my associate, Jerry Pike."

Mr. Pike gave her a bright smile, which showcased a missing front tooth. "How do you do, Miss Lady?" Tesha couldn't help but smile back at the friendly man.

Fred Shanty held a clipboard held together with duct tape in one hand and pulled a long tape measure from a holster that swung low on his hip, and under his belly with the other.

It took several hours for them to walk through the down stairs. While Tesha explained what she wanted, he took notes and made suggestions. Most of what he suggested surprised her. Mr. Shanty obviously knew his stuff, which impressed her.

Jerry Pike mostly poked at fixtures and tsked while mumbling under his breath. Once they returned to the front room, she promised to call him with her decision once she met with her two other contractors.

After Mr. Shanty left, leaving her a crumpled estimate, she went to the kitchen and poured a glass of tea. From her kitchen window, she glanced across the way toward Adam Ford's house. She'd not seen him since he'd walked over to talk about the garden.

He'd left on Saturday morning. Tesha supposed to his parents' house for the weekend and returned sometime during the night.

Although she'd considered driving to Atlanta, to visit her own mom over the weekend, her mother insisted it was not necessary as she'd already planned a spa trip with a friend thanks to a gift certificate Tesha had gifted her. Since her mother kept busy, it was best to preplan visits since it was hit and miss whether or not the social butterfly and travel aficionado would be in town.

Again Tesha peered out the window toward Adam's house. Something didn't feel right.

The black F250 was in the driveway. He'd returned from visiting his parents, it must have been sometime in the middle of the night. She'd not seen him outside much since moving in and it occurred to her that perhaps it was his way to remain inside. After all, the realtor had described him as a recluse. Besides, it was not her place to worry over her neighbor, or to attempt to bring any sort of therapy into his life. If anyone needed help it was her.

Tesha let out a sigh at realizing that the decision to move to Lovely was already helping. The ache in the center of her chest every time her mind wandered to David was as sharp as ever, but thankfully it happened with less frequency now. New projects, the plans for the garden, and admittedly her handsome neighbor were wonderful distractions from the constant grieving her life had become.

LATER THAT DAY, Tesha couldn't believe her crappy luck. The second contractor she'd planned to interview didn't show up, and the third called and cancelled not bothering to set up a follow up appointment. Fuming, she got in her truck to head to town. Hating to waste an entire day, she decided to get some things checked off her endless 'to-do' list. It was only four o'clock in the afternoon. The hardware store would still be open.

She'd already started stripping wallpaper in one of the

smaller rooms downstairs. It would be her pet project for now. One that would take a few days to complete and allow her to get something accomplished while meeting with contractors and such. Once the walls were touched up, she planned to paint in soothing tones and turn the room into her office. It would be her base of operations for all the renovations to come.

Unable to shake the feeling of something strange happening at Adam's house, she turned right instead of left and slowed her car to pass his house. It was too early to see if any lights were on inside, especially with every window covered with closed blinds.

Since he parked on the driveway on the side of his house, she assumed it allowed him to enter through a back door. The truck was a sure sign he was at home.

With a huff, Tesha sped away. It was ridiculous really. It was one thing to check on a neighbor when feeling sure something was wrong, but if she were totally honest with herself, his safety was not her true motivation. The thought of catching a glimpse of the hot guy was. For goodness sakes, she'd only met him a few days earlier and already she was obsessing.

THE BELL JINGLED as Tesha stepped through the doorway of Miller's Hardware. Even with the bright fluorescent lighting that shined from the ceiling it felt old timey. Although not a very large store, every shelf was stocked in an orderly fashion. On the front end of each aisle, signs informed shoppers to its contents. With the size of the town, she figured no one read the signs anymore, knowing the locations by heart.

She neared a counter to the right of the entryway where an older woman held up a flyswatter with a huge fuchsia silk flower glued onto the flat end. Her sharp eyes flashed to Tesha. "Have you ever seen something so gaudy in your life?"

"No, ma'am." Tesha wrinkled her nose. "If you kill a bug with it, it will ruin the flower."

"Who in their right mind wants a decorated flyswatter? My sister Marlene sent me this. She's a nut job."

The woman moved away from the counter and shrank about half a foot. She'd been standing on a small stool. Shaking her head, she made her way to the side of the counter and flung the offensive item into a trashcan. "I have to figure out how to tell her these contraptions won't be gracing my shelves. I don't care if she made a hundred of them. She wasted her time."

Tesha giggled. "I hope she won't be too upset."

The woman wagged her finger at Tesha. "She needs a better hobby than making ugly crap."

With that, she lifted a box to rest on her hip and tottered way.

"Where is your spackle?" Tesha followed the surprisingly quick moving woman. "I also need to get some paint strips."

The store was silent for a few seconds. Tesha looked around and turned in a full circle as she gauged where the woman could have disappeared.

A muffled cursed was followed by the lady coming back up the aisle. "Damn box fell apart." The tiny woman smiled up at Tesha and held out her hand. "Where are my manners? I assume everyone knows me, but you don't. I'm Tallulah Miller."

"Nice to meet you. I'm Tesha Washington." They shook hands.

Mrs. Miller studied Tesha for a short moment. "You're the young woman who bought that house on Magnolia Street, next door to Adam Ford. Well, aren't you just as cute as a button? Come on, I'll show you where the paint section is."

Tesha liked Mrs. Miller immediately. Although she was older, it was hard to tell her age. Her dark brown hair was streaked with silver and her face had few wrinkles. She followed the woman while scanning the shelves for items she might need.

Soft classical music played, giving the air of a forgotten time. "How long have you lived here, Mrs. Miller?"

Waving a hand in the air in a circular motion, Mrs. Miller shook her head. "Since I came here to find my wonderful husband. I'll have to tell you all about it over tea one day. It's been about twenty-eight years now that I came to Lovely. Four since Mr. Miller died, and I took over the store."

The pang in her chest at realizing their common bond made Tesha slow down. She studied the older woman as she hummed and swayed with the music in front of the paint strips. "I love the colorful array don't you? It reminds me of the many choices we make in life and how each one has the ability to make us happy." She winked at Tesha and then pointed to a shelf across from the display. "There's the spackle. Holler if you need anything."

The front door jingled twice, and Mrs. Miller smiled widely. "More friends." In the blink of an eye, she headed away.

Tesha studied the array of shades. The last time she'd picked paint colors was after she and David purchased their

Atlanta townhouse. Her hand moved over the strips, not seeing them, but remembering how he'd pulled bright colors from the slots urging her to choose something crazy.

Admittedly, she'd made a lot of progress since her husband's death, yet each time she thought about him, time moved backwards. How she missed his easy smiles and the mischievous lift at the corner of his lips when teasing her. Almost three years without his touch, their wild lovemaking and other times when they'd cuddled on the couch, watching movies. The memories brought it all back, so it seemed like only yesterday she'd lost him. The war had stolen so much from her.

"What grieves you, sweetheart?" Mrs. Miller stood next to her, the woman's kind gaze taking in her tears.

Tesha hadn't realized tears had fallen as she stood in front of the paint swatches. "I miss my husband." Not sure why she'd blurted the truth, Tesha gasped and covered her mouth.

A warm hand covered her shoulder. "How long has it been?"

"It's strange. I lost him two years ago, but sometimes it seems like only days. Silly things like this." She motioned to the display. "Bring back strong memories of him." Tesha wiped at the tears. "God, I miss him so much."

Mrs. Miller took her hand and led her to a small room behind the front counter. The quaintness of it immediately helped ease her mind away from her sorrow. The walls were covered with colorful wallpaper. The print was of stripes in green, russet, and crème. Two Queen Anne chairs upholstered in another soft floral fabric flanked a painted off-white table that held a beautiful electric teapot, tea bags, and two cups inverted on their saucers. "What a beautiful space," Tesha said and sniffed loudly.

"Well, you sit right down and have a cup of tea. Take as long as you need, sweetie. If I get a break I'll come and join you." There was understanding in Mrs. Miller's gaze as she patted her arm. "It will get better. I bet already there are times when you think of him and smile."

"Yes, I do," Tesha replied with a watery smile. "He made me laugh a lot."

AN HOUR LATER, Tesha drove away from the hardware store. She'd promised to meet Mrs. Miller and her friends for tea soon and actually looked forward to getting to know her new friend better.

Once on her street, she drove past her own house to slow in front of Adam's. Nothing had changed. The blinds were closed, still no lights on that she could see.

It was none of her business, Tesha told herself all the while pulling to a stop and getting out of her small truck. She trotted up the front stairs and pushed the doorbell. Her heart accelerated and she wondered what she'd say if he opened the door.

The two tones of the doorbell sounded hollow inside the house foyer. Would it be rude to try again? Tesha looked around despite the fact there was no house except hers from which anyone could spy her here. She tried the doorknob, and it was locked. Once more she pushed the doorbell and put her ear against the door.

Bong. Bong.

She let out a sigh and placed her palm against the wood of

the door. Unsure why she'd even come, Tesha returned to her truck. If anything she should be grateful he didn't answer, what would she have said? *Hello Adam, just making sure you're alive?*

A thought occurred as she made a U-turn to her own home. What if Adam had a girlfriend? He could be 'entertaining' and here she was interrupting. She let out a huff and then giggled at the reaction. She'd never acted so aggressively over a man. Why did she now?

It was absolutely none of her business what Adam Ford did. Yet as she climbed the stairs to her front door, she took one more look toward his house.

FOR A WEEK now, the sounds of hammering and low masculine voices were familiar. The contractors had been working on her entryway and large front room walls.

In a smaller adjoining area, Tesha rolled the cream-colored paint onto the wall in her soon to be completed office. She'd chosen to paint stripes in two tones, off-white and buttery yellow and it was shaping up well. Another country song started from the larger front room where Mr. Shanty, and his assistant Jerry Pike who hummed off key, worked.

Tesha joined in and whistled along with the quick tempo while painting.

Since she was alone in the room she began to sway in time with the music, wiggling her hips side to side. She may as well paint and get exercise at the same time.

"Hello."

The deep voice startled her and she swung around so fast, the roller landed squarely in the middle of Adam's broad chest. He looked down and then back up to her face, his right eyebrow lifted.

"Oh my God," Tesha moved back and then closed her eyes in embarrassment as her butt squished against the wet wall. "Crud." She put the roller down and grabbed a towel. "Its water based, should come out in the wash if we throw it in now." With quick strokes, she wiped at the paint spot on his chest only managing to make the stain bigger. "I will pay for it of course."

"No need. It's an old t-shirt," Adam replied, his gaze following her movements. Once again she was struck by how he maintained a neutral expression despite the situation. "I came to see what you needed when you stopped by the other day."

He'd been home. Now what to say?

His face was drawn, with dark circles under his eyes and the presence of a beard made her wonder how long it'd been since he'd slept or shaved. Catching herself, she cleared her throat and lifted her shoulders. "Nothing important. I—I…okay honestly, I was checking to make sure you were all right."

Something flashed in his eyes, but he remained quiet.

At a lack of what to say, she motioned around the room. "What do you think? I've always been a fan of two-toned walls. The subtle color difference and one being flat and the other glossy add a texture variance as well." He studied the walls, giving her an opportunity to take him in.

What had been a flat stomach was concave. It gave her the impression he'd not eaten in days. "It looks good." Once again the words were flat, nothing in his expression giving away what he really thought.

In her gut, she knew something was terribly wrong, but with his impenetrable walls, she'd not ask. Instead, Tesha automatically came up with a plan to feed him. Whatever reason kept him from answering the door, the cause of his appearance, she may never know, but she'd do what she could to help.

The look in his eyes, the lack of emotion reminded her of the first days after David's death. Her mother had commented on how the hollow look was painful to look upon. Adam radiated pain.

"Would you mind going with me to grab a bite? I'm starving and have no idea where to get a good home cooked style meal. I've been surviving on thrown together sandwiches and salads."

"I know where you can go." His reply made it obvious he did not plan to accompany her.

Tesha frowned. "You don't want to come?"

His eyes shifted away, the pensive expression on the handsome man's face made her want to grab his face and soothe him. "I'm not much for going out to eat."

"How about we get it to go and eat it outside somewhere. Back here maybe. Come on. I'm so tired of eating alone. I have a picnic table in my future garden space. Just you and me?" She was not about to give up.

His shoulders lowered and his face visibly relaxed. "There a place just past town, they make good barbeque and everything to go along with it."

Tesha searched for the number on her phone and called in

an order. "Meet me out front in five minutes. I have to change my shorts." She dashed from the room not giving him time to change his mind.

Chapter Four

ADAM PAUSED INSIDE his front door waiting for the panic to reappear. When it didn't, he felt assured in venturing out with Tesha.

A smile threatened at recalling her perky butt shaking to the music. He'd not expected the added treat of her having to touch him after painting his chest. Adam pulled the T-shirt over his head and held it up. Instead of throwing it into the wash, he carefully placed it over the back of a chair to dry.

She'd come to check on him. Thank God he'd locked the door and closed all the blinds. The last thing he needed was for her or anyone to appear in the midst of one of his attacks. He didn't want to know what he was capable of in the middle of one of his flashbacks if he imagined her to be an Afghani rebel.

Not wanting to miss his five-minute deadline, he yanked a second t-shirt on and went back out.

Tesha stood by her small truck. She'd changed her grey shorts for a pair of jean cut-offs and on her feet she wore flat sandals. Although he pretended to look at her face, he took in her sweet tight body and felt his own react. *No. Off limits.*

Half an hour later they sat on the picnic bench beside her house eating in quiet accompaniment. He appreciated how she didn't bombard him with questions, but instead spoke of her upcoming projects and on occasion asked his opinion.

She'd bought enough barbeque to feed ten people. He couldn't help but eat more than his fill. Just the smell of the food and her easy company brought out a hunger after not eating for several days.

Shanty and Jerry Pike had also eaten and were now back inside. Tesha was a thoughtful person. It seemed in her nature to care about others. She insisted they sit and eat, fussing over the men when they claimed to be full, pushing extra servings onto their plates.

Her beautiful eyes slid to him. "I apologize for coming over and bothering you the other day. I promise I wasn't trying to be the nosy neighbor. Just had a strange feeling right here." She pushed the side of her fist on her stomach.

It felt good that she'd cared about his well-being, but at the same time, it could be dangerous for her. "I am not always in the mood for company."

Hurt flashed in her eyes and her lips wobbled into an unconvincing smile. "I understand." It was obvious she didn't.

"Tell me about your plans for the garden."

She immediately brightened. "I met Mrs. Miller yesterday. She's going to help me with it."

"Mrs. Miller has a well maintained garden at her house. You should go look at it. She spends most of her time there when she's not at the store."

Tesha smiled. He took a deep breath wondering how a simple thing like a smile from this woman affected him so deeply. "I am going there for tea one of these days. She's introducing me to other widows. It's perfect for my plans for this house."

Widow?

"You're a widow?"

She took a deep breath and released it slowly. Adam rushed to speak again. "You don't have to tell me."

"It's fine. Yes, I lost my husband in Iraq."

The mention of that country made his jaw clench, but he managed to relax for her sake. "I'm sorry."

"No need to apologize. If anything I should thank you for what you did over there. The real estate agent told me you are a war vet." Before he could say anything, she changed the subject. "How was your mom's birthday? Did they enjoy the lasagna?"

"It went well." He didn't want to talk anymore. There were too many things better left unsaid. Adam got to his feet. "Let's walk. I ate too much."

It was clear she knew he was avoiding conversation because Tesha cocked her head to the side as if considering what to say. In the end she got to her feet. "Sure. Let me throw these paper plates in the trash."

He helped her carry the leftovers and glasses inside and they set off. It was a sunny day, only a few puffy clouds in the sky. His dark wraparound shades covered his eyes and gave him ample opportunity to glimpse at his companion without her knowing. She pointed to a Victorian across the street from their houses. "Who lives there?"

"Aaron Reginald Moore. The Moore's are the founding family of Lovely. The town is actually named after his great-grandmother, Lovely Elizabeth Moore."

"I'd love to see the inside. Do you think he'd be open to let me?" She stood in the middle of the street and looked up at the imposing three-story home. "Don't you just love the creativi-

37

ty?" Bright eyed and smiling she turned to him. "I'm going to walk over one day and introduce myself."

A corner of his mouth twitched, a smile threatening. He shrugged. "I'm sure he will be happy to show you the interior. He entertains a lot. Always has folks over."

They continued walking past the house. The next area was mostly wooded. Adam explained it was part of the Walker's property. Then there were smaller houses that lined both sides of the road for the next two miles the road stretched into town.

Tesha touched his hand to get his attention. Adam could not help the flash of heat traveling from the spot directly to the center of his body. "I thought we were taking a leisurely walk, not going on a race."

Although she was only a bit out of breath, he noted perspiration on her brow. He slowed. "Didn't realize I was walking so fast."

"Maybe not for you, but I'm a foot shorter." She laughed at his frown. "I don't mind exercise, but I ate too much to jog."

Spending time with the pretty woman made him yearn for more. He wanted to know what it would be like to hold her against him, the taste of her kisses. If she were not his neighbor, he'd definitely sleep with her. But getting to know her and the proximity of their homes made her strictly off limits. Then there was the obvious situation with her being widowed in the same war that sent him stateside with demons he fought constantly.

Plus there was the added complication of the man with the Camaro who'd been there the day she moved in. What role did he play?

Sirens screamed in the distance and got louder. The emergency vehicle was headed toward them. Adam searched frantically for a place to go. The louder the sounds, the more frantic he became. He had to get away from Tesha. If a flashback occurred, he'd never want to face her again. As the ambulance neared, Tesha grabbed his arm and leaned against him. "Oh my goodness. It's coming this way. There are only four houses on our little street."

When his breathing and heart rate accelerated, Adam wrapped his arms around Tesha and held her as the ambulance zoomed past them. Her slight body against his took over any thoughts other than wanting her and he relaxed into her.

"Let's see if there's something we can do to help." She gave him a quizzical look and shrugged from his hold. Without a word, she took his hand tugging him to return.

"I'm not sure what I'm going to do now." An hour later, Tesha sat on the front steps, her chin resting on her palms. "Poor Mr. Shanty."

Fred Shanty had passed out. Although he'd come to and insisted the paramedics leave him be, he'd been carted off to Lovely Medical Center.

Jerry Pike followed the ambulance in the dilapidated truck after assuring Tesha he'd be back to help as much as he could with the renovations until Mr. Shanty recovered.

Adam kicked at a small rock and shoved his hands into his jean's pockets. "I'll be here tomorrow to help you."

Her rounded eyes lifted to him. "Thank you so much, but you don't have to. If you do however, I'll pay you."

His chest expanded and he felt like a true hero. "No need, that's what neighbors are for."

"I insist," Tesha told him, her raised eyebrows challenging. "I'll see you in the morning."

Tomorrow he'd have to tell her the conditions of his help. Somehow convince her she'd have to keep her distance from him at all times.

EARLY THE NEXT day Adam arrived at Tesha's house, just as she hurried out the door with a bagel in between her teeth. She waved him in and pointed to Jerry Pike, who sat on a paint stained barstool in the kitchen drinking coffee and eating a bagel. He went to the counter and poured a cup of coffee.

Jerry Pike washed down his food with the coffee. "Shanty's gonna be all right. Just needs to rest is all." The older man became sullen. "Sure am glad you stepped in to help. Not sure how long 'fore Shanty makes it back and 'Lil Bit needs these wall done 'fore summer hits."

"Can I ask that you keep your distance and warn me before you do something that will create a loud noise?" Adam waited for Jerry Pike to begin asking questions.

Instead the man shrugged and nodded. "You got it."

"Thanks."

The older man sized Adam up. "Yer that fella who came back from Afghanistan a couple years ago right?"

"Yes."

"You brought it back with ya, too. I know the feelin'." He didn't elaborate, but Adam figured the man must have served sometime in the past.

Once they started working, Adam realized Jerry was a great assistant. Did as he was told without complaint and adjusted to Adam's pace every step of the way. As long as the country music played, Jerry Pike seemed impervious to hard work.

At noon, Jerry Pike unhooked his tool belt and placed it on top of a crate. "Well, I'm goin' to town to check on Shanty. I'll be back in an hour or so." He walked away humming to the music.

How many people could see it?

Adam threw a dirty rag into a bucket deciding to take a break as well. He peered into the room Tesha had been working on. The painting was done. His gaze went to the spot where she'd backed into the wall. The paint on her butt had gained not only his attention, but the awareness of how attracted he was to her.

Sometime later, the crunching of tires told of Tesha's return. Adam decided this was the time to tell her that if they were ever alone, it was best for her to keep a distance. He was not looking forward to disclosing his issues, but at the same time, hurting her was not an option. If there was any chance of getting to know her better, it would end with this conversation.

She entered and immediately stopped in her tracks upon seeing him. "Oh, hi, I thought everyone was gone."

His stomach pitched when their eyes met. "I need to talk to you." The room seemed to shrink considerably when she walked in.

Her gaze shifted past him. "Do I need to sit for this? You're not going to quit on me already are you?"

"No."

Tesha went to a chair and fell into it. She lowered the bag she carried to the floor. Her lips curved up. "Oh, good. It's been one of those days. I got a flat tire and then the hardware store was closed, so I drove an hour away to get these." She pulled silver light switch cover from the bag. "Thank goodness it matches the ones I already got."

Before he could begin speaking, she dashed to the wall and held the item up to compare. "Perfect."

God how the woman attracted him, she pulled at his every sense. Adam gripped his hands behind his back and looked past her to the doorway. He should leave, walk out and not return. What was he thinking being there? Yes, this was crazy. He'd tell her it wasn't going to work. Walk away now before he did something stupid. Even if she didn't understand, it was better than telling her the truth, that one more minute around her would result in more than just talking.

Adam neared and swallowed, forming the words he'd say. Her perfume tickled his nose and he inhaled deeper. Without thought he reached to touch her hair. When she turned and found him so close, her eyes widened and lips parted. Her regard fell to his lips.

Aw hell. He cupped the back of her neck and leaned forward, his intent obvious. He closed in, his eyes locking with hers. Tesha reached up and pulled on his shoulder granting permission.

Not needing further encouragement, he covered her mouth with his. The softness of her lips was intoxicating, so sweet. With an exhalation, she relaxed, her body fitting perfectly against him.

He intensified the kiss, running his tongue across the center of her lips and nipping at the corners. Her arms circled around his neck, which brought her soft breasts flat against his chest. The sensation of her fingers raking through his hair stole every ounce of his self-control.

The sounds of their kissing and heavy breathing mixed with the soft country music in the background. His large palms cupped her butt and he lifted Tesha to let her feel his arousal. Tesha moaned and wrapped her legs around his waist.

The obvious attraction between them blossomed into instant chemistry like he'd never experience before. If the world ended at the moment, neither would be able to pull away from the other.

He wanted all of her, to taste every inch and take everything she'd give him. For the first time in his life, he understood pure raw need. The overwhelming demands to be with someone and never let go.

Tesha was against the wall, Adam held her up with ease as he feasted on her mouth and lips, enjoying the tangle of their tongues. A battle he would not have a problem losing. He was hard and throbbing from the heat of her center against his groin.

A rumble became louder and louder. Tesha pushed him away. "Oh goodness, Jerry's here."

Adam moved away, his chest heaving. He adjusted his jeans, in an attempt to hide his erection. Tesha hurried out of the room, rushed to the next one and closed the door.

"Yo? Anyone here?"

After blowing out a breath, Adam went to the front room. "I'm here."

Jerry Pike made a beeline for the radio and turned the music up and looked over at him. "You have been working hard, look all sweaty." He narrowed his eyes. "What happened to your hair?"

"I think I'm done for the day."

Chapter Five

TESHA REMAINED IN her bedroom for the rest of the day until the sounds of hammering stopped and Jerry Pike called out that he was leaving. The silence of the house combined with her grumbling stomach led her in search of something to eat.

It was inevitable. Her gaze darted to the room where she and Adam shared the most incredible kiss of her life. She'd sat on her bed waiting for guilt to assault, for tears to appear at betraying David, like when she'd been intimate with Cleve, but instead, she'd grinned like an idiot.

How incredible his large body had felt against hers. He'd picked her up and kissed her with so much hunger. Desperation was the only word she could use to describe it.

The same feelings had echoed within her. So much want. Incredible intoxicating need. A fire burning so hot she'd expected to burn to ashes before he was done.

It would be a long night. In the morning she'd see him again and hopefully they'd agree the kiss was great, but a mistake. It was not a good idea to date a next-door neighbor.

Then again. She leaned on the counter and drank her tea while looking toward Adam's house. "No. No. No. Stop it, Tesha."

The lights were on tonight. What was he doing?

THE FIRST SOUND of hammering woke Tesha. Jerry Pike always arrived early. Way too early. She opened one eye and looked at the clock. Seven in the morning. Good God, did that man not know most people slept in? Tesha rolled toward the wall and pulled the blankets over her head. She'd not slept a wink, when she'd finally fallen asleep the dream was of her and Adam and not much else. She'd become so frustrated, even her vibrator pissed her off when it couldn't take the edge off.

Now he'd be out there and she'd have to face him. Hopefully he'd not be able to see how badly she wanted him. That would be embarrassing. Thankfully he had no way of knowing the naughty things they'd done in her dreams. Her body instantly reacted to the reminder. "Augh!" Tesha growled and pulled the pillow over her face.

Unable to avoid it any longer, she left her bedroom after ensuring her makeup was perfect and every single strand of hair in place. Wearing a loose-fitting University of Georgia t-shirt and leggings along with a pair of running shoes, she was prepared to face him.

Adam stopped mid-sentence when she appeared. His eyes followed her as she made her way to the kitchen. "Good morning, gentlemen." Tesha took in both men who watched her with very different expressions. Jerry expecting breakfast and all she could see in Adam's gaze was the usual flatness.

It annoyed her to no end how the man could remain so neutral. Even when kissing he'd remained quiet, only his body communicating with her.

She cleared her throat and made a point to look at Jerry. "I'm making ham and cheese biscuits. My specialty."

Once she tied her favorite apron around her waist, Tesha

became lost in cooking. One of the reasons she couldn't wait to open a Bed and Breakfast was the opportunity to cook for others. She enjoyed trying out new recipes especially breakfast creations.

Adam came to stand next to her as she rolled out the biscuit dough. "We need to talk."

"You said that yesterday and that's not what happened. Although your tongue was moving pretty good." She couldn't help but tease him. When she slid her gaze to his face, she noticed he'd colored a bit. "I like how you talk to me."

He fidgeted but as usual remained silent. Tesha took pity on him. "The biscuits will be done in about ten minutes. After we eat, then we can talk. All right?"

"Yes." His frown made her worry about their talk. But then he squeezed her upper arm before turning away.

A FEW HOURS later, Tesha sat outside on her deck. Adam came outside and looked down at her. "There is something I need to make clear." Adam's words did not bode well. Tesha prepared for the "I have a girlfriend" speech.

"What is it, Adam?" She stretched her arms over her head to give the impression of nonchalance while her stomach did a fast tap dance.

He swallowed visibly. "If we're in the house alone while I work. It's best if you keep your distance. I can react violently to unexpected noises or people coming up to me when I don't expect it." His serious gaze met hers. "Promise you'll never sneak up on me. And if I leave in a hurry, don't come after me." He took a breath, and she realized talking about this took a lot out of him.

PTSD. He had Post Traumatic Stress Disorder and wanted to protect her. So this was the reason why he was a recluse and why he was not comfortable around people.

Tesha's heart broke for him. It didn't take much to recognize Adam had been a leader in the military. He stood out as a pure alpha male who must have commanded attention and respect. That he could barely function in public now, had to be debilitating, hard to accept. "I promise."

"Good. That's good." Adam took a step backward his eyes boring into hers. "Tesha, please understand that nothing can ever happen between us. I am not ready for…"

Now he made her angry, how dare he assume she was all ga-ga over him from just one kiss?

Even if she was a little bit more than interested in him. How dare he assume it? She'd kept it cool this morning, barely looking at him and had actually managed to convince herself not to be tempted by him. But the gall of the man to think she found him so irresistible, he had to warn her away. "I expect nothing and I'm not going to fall at your feet in adoration just because of a kiss. You don't have to warn me off."

She jumped to her feet and absolutely hated how much shorter than him she was. With quick jabs, she pushed her finger into the center of his chest. "It was just a kiss, Adam Ford. Shit happens." Tesha stomped off to the house. *The nerve of the man.*

But, why the hell did her feelings get hurt at his words?

BY THAT AFTERNOON her back ached from peeling wallpaper in what would be her bedroom. Admittedly Tesha had overdone it. Amazing how much she'd gotten done fueled by anger and whatever other emotions propelled her all day.

The wallpaper stripping was finished. The next day she'd start priming the walls for paint.

The second floor didn't need much work. Surprisingly, each room had been kept in great shape. All she planned to do was paint the bedrooms and decorate in different themes.

There was an adjoining bathroom between two of the bedrooms and the third had its own. The bathrooms would be fitted with new fixtures and cabinetry. In her mind's eye, she pictured how beautiful the end result would be. Each one a special haven for her guests.

Outside the window a silver car got her attention. She yanked the bandana off her head and rushed downstairs to meet her friend.

"Cleve!" Tesha ran into his arms and hugged his waist tight. "I missed you so much."

She was aware that both Adam and Jerry had stopped working and stared at them. Not ready to face Adam, she took Cleve's hand and pulled him into the house and straight to her office. "Sit down, let's chat. I'll show you around later. You'll be amazed at all the progress that's been made."

Cleve smiled and looked the room over. "It already looks great. I forget how good you are at this sometimes."

He sat and crossed his long legs at the ankles. Dressed casually in jeans and a tight black t-shirt that showed off his well-toned physique, he looked incredible. Tesha wondered why she didn't feel more than just sisterly love for the handsome man. "What brings you to little ol' Lovely?"

"You, of course," Cleve replied with a flirty smile. "Can't go long without checking on my girl."

Tears sprung at his words, she'd not realized how lonely she'd been without her circle of friends. "How are Susie, Phil, and Amanda doing?"

"Honestly I haven't seen them much since you left. We're planning to do after work drinks later this week, but without you to corral us, we are a lost lot." He laughed. "I'll be surprised if we do meet this coming week."

Tesha let out a breath. "Let's go to town and have lunch. I have so much to tell you. I want to hear all about what you've been doing."

Cleve motioned around the room. "Great. I'll look around while you get dressed."

"Good idea. I'll be back in a few minutes. I'll just jump in the shower and change. Help yourself to a drink, the frig is stocked."

Tesha hurried past the men who'd resumed working. Once in her bedroom she closed the door. It would be nice to spend time with Cleve, to forget about the house and be away from Adam for a bit. Although she knew he'd not meant to hurt her feelings, it was hard not be angry with him. To admit to herself, she had expected more from their encounter. She was madly attracted to the man and it wasn't his fault.

Chapter Six

THE HAMMER LANDED squarely on his thumb. Adam let out a ripe curse that had more to do with his mood than the pain. Jerry Pike glanced over, but seemed to sense he'd not welcome any sympathy.

Tesha's friend however was not as insightful. The man who somehow managed to look overdressed in a t-shirt and jeans, neared. "Ow, that's gotta hurt. Want some ice?"

When he glared at him, the guy shrugged and walked down the hallway towards Tesha's bedroom. Adam narrowed his eyes at the retreating man's back. For whatever reason the Cleve character kept moving past her door, the entire time examining the walls and peering into rooms. Inspecting the workmanship no doubt. Adam had a hard time picturing the guy holding a hammer, much less installing drywall.

Tesha emerged wearing a short yellow sundress and sandals. A tiny strap slipped off her shoulder. He remembered pressing his lips to the exact spot. Her eyes met his at that moment, as if she read his thoughts, she pulled the errant strap into place.

She looked away. "Cleve?"

Cleve? Really, what kind of a name was that? The guy appeared through a doorway. Together they went into a back room. Not wanting to overhear them, he began to hammer nails into the wall one after the other.

A few moments later, the couple returned. From the corner of his eyes, Adam took Tesha in. Her hair was in place, her lip color intact. What an idiot her boyfriend was. After all these days apart, he'd not kissed her yet. Adam ignored the sense of relief at knowing he'd been the last one to kiss Tesha.

She paused behind them. "Jerry, Adam, this is my friend, Cleve."

Jerry did not hesitate to shake hands with her friend. Adam simply nodded at the guy, thankful for the hammer and nails he held.

Tesha gave him a befuddled look. Maybe she feared her boyfriend would find out about the kiss. "We'll be back late so I'll see you both tomorrow then."

He couldn't be a jerk to her. "See you tomorrow."

They left in Cleve's car.

"They make a handsome couple, don't you think?" Jerry asked and resumed humming.

"Yeah, handsome," Adam grumbled under his breath.

He wondered if the guy was spending the night.

THAT EVENING, HIS house loomed empty and dark as he moved around the kitchen. He'd not cooked much since he'd begun helping Tesha. Admittedly since having a reason to get up every morning, he'd felt better, no flashbacks or nightmares in over a week.

The doorbell rang and he wondered if it was Tesha. No one else ever visited. His brothers didn't count. They came in without knocking, each having a key to the house. When he opened the door instant regret at not looking through the peephole first slammed him.

Valerie, his ex-wife, strolled past him not bothering to utter a greeting. She swung her long blond hair behind her shoulder and placed a hand on her hip. Valerie was tall, thin, and very attractive. Her shrewd green eyes scanned the surroundings before returning to him.

"How are you, babe? I ran into Jensen in L.A. He told me you'd moved here. I am worried sick, had to rush over to make sure you hadn't totally lost your mind."

She didn't seem worried, much less sick. "I'm sure Jensen would have told you if I had."

He was going to kill his brother. They'd seen each other at their parents' home, just a week earlier and Jenson hadn't mentioned running into Valerie. Then again, being the hottest leading man at the moment, Jenson Ford was in high demand. His brother jetted from one city to the next. Probably didn't think it important if he even remembered.

Valerie's heels clacked on the wooden floors as she moved to the kitchen. Once she placed what was no doubt an exorbitantly expensive purse on the counter she perched on a barstool. She took in the empty space. "I can recommend a decorator."

Before returning from Afghanistan, he wondered many times what he'd feel when seeing Valerie again. The letter ending their marriage was delivered to him at the medical unit right after he was shot and flown with the other injured men to safety.

After he read the letter, it became a battle of what hurt worst, the wounds or her betrayal. Now three years later, he realized with relief, the only thing he felt at the moment was apathy.

"Does your television executive know you're visiting me?"

She gave him an indulgent smile. "I am not seeming him any longer. Didn't Jenson tell you?"

"He didn't mention you at all."

Valerie attempted to hide the surprise of his statement by rolling her eyes. But he knew her well enough to have seen it when she'd inhaled and frowned for a second.

"Yes, well, it was a mistake. After everything was said and done, I found out he was a farce. His series was cancelled and the network let him go for unspecified reasons."

"Your gravy train dried up." Adam almost laughed. He retrieved two beers knowing she'd balk at drinking from a bottle. "Beer?"

"You know I don't drink beer."

She rounded the counter and neared him. With an upward curve to her perfectly painted lips, Valerie ran her hands up his arms. The familiar aroma of her expensive perfume reminded him of better days with her. Of a time when she'd professed loving him. A *love* that ended when he'd decided to join the military. Although they didn't need the money since his investments continued to earn more than his Army pay, she hated losing the social status of being a CEO's wife.

"Adam, let's try again. I never stopped loving you, not really. I made a mistake. You and I had a good thing. Our relationship deserves a second chance, don't you think?" She cupped his face with both hands. "I missed you terribly."

"I've been back for almost three years."

"I know. It's just that it wasn't until I saw Jenson did I find out where you were. You changed your phone number and moved. I called two of your other brothers. Tristan said some horrible things and Jensen hung up on me."

He'd have to remember to buy his brothers a drink next time they got together. "I'm not interested, Valerie."

"Are you seeing someone?" She blinked up at him attempting to draw tears. "If so, I am sure you'll never feel about anyone like you did about me."

"I was a busy executive at the time, Valerie. Too blinded by your beauty and supposed feelings to analyze what exactly I felt."

"You are hurting me." Valerie finally succeeded in producing a tear. "I won't believe you stopped loving me. I refuse to."

He stepped away and drank deeply from the beer. Then motioned to the dining room table. "I was about to eat. You're welcome to join me."

"I'll have to stay the night regardless. I didn't see anything other than a grimy roadside motel within hours of here." She went back to the barstool. "Do you have any wine?"

She'd attempt to seduce him. It would be a colossal mistake to sleep with his ex-wife, not just because she'd come up with some ridiculous reason to remain longer, but also because it would send mixed signals. No, it was better not to prolong an already bad situation.

Since the kiss with Tesha, his body had not stopped demanding release. However, release would not come with his ex-wife. His body might not be selective, but he was.

THEY MANAGED TO make it past the evening meal. Valerie did not relent, constantly bringing up things they'd done together, hinted at their lovemaking while flirting the entire time.

Dinner parties, travel to the Caribbean, jaunts to Napa Valley. It could have all been a movie. The Adam Ford who lived that life no longer existed.

The doorbell rang and this time he prayed it would not be Tesha. He ignored it until Valerie stood. "I'll get it."

"No." He moved past her. "Sit, finish your wine."

Tesha looked up when he opened the door. He would have groaned, but held it in. She still wore the enticing yellow sundress. With a timid smile held up a small basket with two muffins. "I made muffins. Cleve loves them. I wanted to give you a check for what I owe you so far and also apologize for earlier…" Her eyes moved past him and widened.

Valerie neared and placed her hand on his shoulder. "They smell amazing, good thing you brought two." She reached for the basket. "Although they are huge, I couldn't possibly eat an entire one."

When Adam did not make to introduce them, Valerie nudged him on the shoulder and giggled. "I apologize for my husband. I'm Valerie Ford." She held out her hand. "He didn't used to be so awkward around people."

Tesha managed to recover enough to shake Valerie's hand. "I'm Tesha Washington. I moved in next door a couple weeks ago."

"Really?" Valerie stuck her head past the doorway and looked towards Tesha's house. "It looks like it needs a lot of work."

Her expression told more than words of her disapproval of the house. "I suppose you got it for a steal."

Tesha took a step back and attempted a smile, but didn't succeed. "I don't want to bother you two. Didn't realize you had company."

"Seems to be a day for unexpected company," Adam replied.

"I surprised him." Valerie kissed his cheek and Adam couldn't make up his mind if Tesha thinking he was married was a good thing or not. It would certainly keep her away and safe.

Valerie however wanted to make sure Tesha understood he was off limits. "Adam and I are discussing renewing our relationship. We've been through a little thing, but our relationship is definitely getting stronger. Isn't it, sweetheart?"

"If you say so." Adam leaned away from Valerie, but she remained plastered against his side. "Thank you, Tesha."

"Oh, I almost forgot. Mr. Shanty returns tomorrow so…" Tesha left the rest of the sentence unsaid. "Anyway, thank you very much, for everything." She hurried down the porch steps and headed home.

Adam didn't bother speaking to Valerie when the door closed. He went straight to his bedroom ignoring her pointed look. He didn't owe her any explanations, of course if anything, it was probably a good thing she'd been there when Tesha appeared.

He was angry and truthfully jealous of the guy who was there alone with Tesha. It tortured him not to be the one who sat in the kitchen and watched her bake while listening to music and possibly dancing for him. She was in a safe albeit strange relationship and now Tesha believed him to be in one as well.

Good.

A growl escaped at admitting to himself how often his

mind wandered to Tesha. More than attraction, he felt an emotion, closer to caring than anything else. Something he could not afford to ever feel.

He glanced at the door and considered locking it. If his ex-wife planned to spend the night, she'd have to figure things out herself. His brothers always managed, so could Valerie. Especially since she'd invited herself.

Through the window he saw lights on downstairs at Tesha's house. The silver Camaro was still present.

What would have happened if Valerie had not been present when she'd come over? Would he have demanded clarification of who the guy, Cleve was? And probably make a total fool of himself. He wondered if Tesha's boyfriend had insisted he pay Adam and tell him not to return. It seemed convenient that Mr. Shanty was returning just after the guy appeared. Perhaps the Cleve guy suspected something.

Adam lay on the bed atop the covers with his head on his hands. Footsteps sounded. Valerie came to his door and opened it. "Adam?"

He grunted in reply. "Go away."

In true Valerie fashion she ignored his reply and entered the room to stand over him. "Can I sleep with you? There aren't any other beds in the house."

"No."

She wore only a bra and panties. "I didn't pack any pajamas." Her lips curved when his gaze scanned over her fit body. "I am yours for the taking. You know that, don't you?" Valerie lowered onto the bed and inched over until she lay next to him. She pressed a kiss to his jaw. "I missed you."

Adam closed his eyes. It would be so easy to give in, to

have sex with her and to hell with the consequences. Why keep from enjoying what she offered? He placed his hand on her hip and looked down at her. "I don't love you."

"But you want me." Valerie slid her hand past his stomach, her fingers surrounding his hardening length. "You're so big, Adam. I miss how good you feel inside me."

Adam rolled over her and pinned her arms over her head and looked down at her. "Why did you leave me?"

"Let's not talk about that now." Her eyes skimmed over his face to his lips. "Kiss me."

He kissed the throbbing vein on the side of her throat. "Tell me."

Valerie moaned and lifted her hips to press herself against his arousal. "You left me. Had to go and join the Army. It was the rashest thing. What was I supposed to do?"

Like being dunked in cold water, he lost all desire and pushed up and away from her. Adam stood and glared down on her. "You never even tried to understand."

"How could I? You're an idiot." Valerie sat up and yanked blankets over herself. "Had to go and be a hero. What did it get you? It didn't bring your friend back, did it? Your friend is dead and the towers are still gone."

Cruel words were Valerie's weapons of choice. Adam gestured to the bed. "You can sleep here. I'll take the couch."

"Fuck you," she screamed as he grabbed a blanket from the closet and went downstairs.

Echoes of the explosion vibrated in the air. Screams and smoke competed with the heat and searing pain surrounding him. Adam's side throbbed, the flesh ripped wide open, sliced by metal and who knew what else. A grimy hand stretched toward him out of the floating, swirling sand and he reached for it. "I can't help you."

More hands appeared, every one begging to be saved and he tried frantically to move toward them, but his feet were so heavy. It felt as if one hundred pound weights were tied around his ankles. Drawing from within, he dragged himself forward inch by inch. When he clutched the first hand, it slipped from his grip. To the right, a dead soldier lay. His unseeing eyes locked to him and seemed to blame him.

He could barely move, his sluggish body refusing to do as his brain commanded. Another soldier appeared. Drenched in blood, the man fell face first onto the ground. An explosion sounded, more screams.

Darkness enveloped, closing over the scene and Adam screamed. Not yet. He had to help them. There were so many hands.

Adam shouted digging into the darkness. "No!" A bright light burst overhead followed by a loud bang. He fell face first onto the ground and covered his head with both arms. "God, make it stop."

A low moan came from his right side. Someone was there he was sure of it. If only he could help them, if only they weren't so far out of his reach. "Where are you?"

There were no replies, no hints to where the wounded lay. How could he help them? Vinnie's face became visible and he hurled forward. "I'm here. Hold on." Tears fell, his eyes burned from the combination of smoke and despair. How was it possible? His friend was dead, yet he seemed alive, his hand *reaching for him while mouthing for help.*

Every muscle trembled from the exertion of dragging himself toward Vinnie, he prayed to make it to his friend in time. Finally he grasped a handful of uniform and yank himself closer until he lay panting over his friend.

"I've got you. I've got you." Adam looked into his friend's eyes. They were still, unseeing, his mouth gaping open, blood oozed from his nose and ears. "No." Adam pressed his forehead against Vinnie's. "Don't leave me."

"No!"

Adam tumbled off the couch and landed on the floor with a loud thump. His heart banged against his sternum with so much force he wondered if it would break free. Air refused to fill his lungs, but he tried again and again to gulp it down. With shaky hands, he grabbed at the sheet tangled around him and wiped the sweat from his face.

The buzzing in his ears was soft but grew louder. He covered them with both hands and scurried to the corner of the room. With his back to the wall, his widened eyes attempted to see into the darkness. Was someone there? The noise was too loud to know for sure, but those hands reached still. The screams although barely audible were there.

"No. No. Stop." He gulped back the cry that threatened when his vision turned red. Streams of blood trailed down the walls in thick ripples and pooled on the floor. He recoiled, but the pool grew wider until he couldn't avoid his feet touching it. "God, please…" Adam rushed to the other side of the room and began to do push-ups, his eyes shut. "One. Two. Three. Four…."

After his arms gave out, he flipped to his stomach and continued with sit-ups, one after the other, exhausting his body. The counting helped some, the visions dimmed until finally they were gone just as the sun crept out, lighting the room with the promise of a new day.

"Adam?" Valerie walked into the kitchen a couple hours later. She'd taken great care with her appearance. Already make up in place and wearing jewelry, she looked ready to head out. Valerie lifted a brow and gazed to where he sat drinking coffee. "Oh, there you are." She paused waiting for him to acknowledge her.

"Leave."

"Why are you so damn mean to me? I came to try and reason with you. I traveled all this way to attempt to work things out." She plopped into a chair opposite him.

Valerie was a beautiful woman, her skin flawless, her features almost perfect. Behind the façade she was without depth, not one speck of caring or sweetness. The world, in her mind, revolved around her.

Adam decided to be blunt. "You left me. It was you who ended things. I have moved on. I don't want to work things out. I want you to go back to L.A. or wherever you live and forget about me."

Her eyes narrowed. "Who is she?"

"What the hell are you talking about?"

"There's someone else isn't there? Surely not that cute girl next door, the plain Jane that came over yesterday."

"Just you and me in this." Adam stood and poured a second cup.

Ignoring him, Valerie opened the refrigerator and peered

in. "I'm going into town. I need food." She rolled her eyes at him. "My flight leaves tomorrow, so I need to stay another night. I'll give you some time alone to reconsider what is a huge mistake. Think about it. We were good together. Very good." Her hand closed over his crotch and he cursed the thin fabric of his sweat pants. "You always felt so good inside me, Adam." Valerie became bolder when his flesh reacted to her touch. Her lips pressed against his.

Adam took her by the shoulders and moved her away. "No."

Relief washed over him when Valerie drove off a few minutes later. He closed his eyes and leaned against the wall.

Another day and she'd be gone. He considered physically kicking her out, and then gave up on the idea. Knowing Valerie, she'd turn it into a case of physical abuse.

After an hour, he decided to drive into town, get out of the house maybe the fresh air would clear his head. When he passed Tesha's house, he noticed the Camaro was gone.

He planned to start work on the backyard and put up a fence. There were plenty of projects on his list to keep him busy. One thing was to enclose a small area just off a screened porch. He had to go get a dog. His friend from the Army, James Malloy, was becoming anxious and called twice the previous week to see if he'd follow through on the promise to pick up a puppy, which he insisted as a gift for saving his life.

The only repayment he needed was Malloy alive, even if on the other end of the phone sounding irritated.

Once the fence was set up, the animal could have run of the area without him having to worry about the pup being a nuisance to neighbors.

His truck rumbled down the road, the wind from the open windows blowing warm against his skin and he looked across the farmland.

It was extremely hard at times to forget that Vince Bailey should be the one there, the one fixing up the house, rebuilding the classic Fairlane in the garage and the one building a fence for a dog. Not him.

Adam served alongside Vince for two years. The guy never stopped talking about his plans for the house, what he was going to do once he left the military.

"I'm gonna fix up the Victorian house so when I bring my future wife there, she'll not have a choice but to fall in love with me." He'd get a faraway look with a wide grin. *"She'll decorate the inside and spend her time gardening and such, while I work on my car or watch a game. My dog's gonna be a German Shepard named Sargent. It will be hanging out with me in the backyard. I have it all planned out. You'll come visit me won't ya, Ford?"*

Adam heard the story so many times while they'd stood guard or attempted to sleep while keeping an ear out in case of attack. Sometimes Vince would go into so much detail that although bored at the time, now Adam didn't have to work hard to make his friend's dream come true. For two years he toiled on the house, got it to look exactly like Vince would've liked.

It was busy downtown so it took him a bit to find a free parking spot two blocks from the hardware store in the center of town. He figured it didn't matter to park a ways away. If the hardware store had the items he needed, then he'd drive around back to load them.

He wondered if Valerie was in town. He walked past one of two eating establishments. The Lovely café was packed with diners. Adam looked at his watch. It was almost one, still lunchtime.

Movement inside caught his attention. A blonde swung her hair. Valerie sat at a booth with her back to him. Sharing the booth was Tesha's boyfriend, Cleve. Neither noticed him so he searched to see if Tesha was in the booth. They looked to be alone. Valerie reached for the man's hand and ran her fingers over his knuckles and in return he smiled at her and said something that made her laugh.

What the hell?

That was it. The woman had no morals. She professed love to him just minutes earlier and now she was trying to hook up with someone else. And the man Cleve didn't seem to have a problem with it. He turned on his heel and went back to his truck.

WHEN VALERIE RETURNED to Adam's house an hour later, he opened the door and placed her overnight bag on the porch. "Leave, Valerie, we're done."

Her expression did not register shock. Instead a mocking smile curved her lips. "I don't need you, Adam. You're crazy to turn me down. I can't believe I wasted my time on you."

"Same here."

Chapter Seven

THE BRISK, EARLY evening air helped cool Tesha's overheated skin. Hopefully the air conditioner would be installed before the weather got hotter. Although the walls were done, the process of getting them painted and making arrangements for a plumber, an electrician, and such was taking longer than she expected. She considered if perhaps it was her only option to find people from Nashville who were willing to travel. One disadvantage of living in a small town was that labor was limited.

Outside in her soon-to-be garden, Tesha held her face up to the full moon. Nights like these she missed David's company the most. He would indulge her love of late evening walks and would accompany her sometimes and hold her hand. He'd walk alongside in silence allowing her the quiet time she needed.

She blinked tears away and narrowed her eyes into the darkness at strange sounds. Bright lights came from the back of Adam's house.

The noise continued. As if someone was dragging a heavy object. It was late for someone to be working. Of course Adam seemed to keep odd hours. There was a thud and then more dragging. Curiosity got the best of her and she crept toward the back of his house.

Out back, Adam stood with his shirt off, facing away from her. It looked as if he'd just dragged two large bundles of wire fencing. He held a tape measure in one hand and scratched his head with the other.

It was comical when he let out a breath and looked up to the sky as if for inspiration. After a few moments, he began measuring the ground, shoving stakes into the dirt.

If he was building some sort of pen, he was missing the fact that it would be best if he moved it closer to the trees on the side of the property. The shade would be helpful to whatever creature he planned to pen. Not only that. The current location divided the yard, making it an awkward space.

"Why don't you tell me what you're thinking?" Tesha jumped when he spoke to her. The sound of his deep voice felt like a caress.

"That you should build it back a ways, closer to the trees so it's shaded when it's sunny and protected from rain and such too." She went to stand near him, ensuring to keep a distance and pointed to where he'd laid a long metal pipe. "Here it will partially block your shed and pathway to the garage."

He stared at her and then looked away. "Your boyfriend didn't stay long?"

Tesha considered letting Adam think she and Cleve were more than friends. But this new start, moving to Tennessee was not going to start with lies. "He's just a friend. We've known each other for years."

"I find it hard to believe the guy never made a move." His interest in her private life was an interesting change. Adam rarely spoke, much less asked questions.

"We dated for a short while, it was...awkward at best. So

we decided we were best suited as friends." Tesha decided since he'd opened the door to step right through. "What about your wife, she's gone. I take it your reconciliation didn't go well."

His mouth tightened, but he seemed to realize it was a fair exchange he'd started. "She is my *ex*-wife and there will never be a reconciliation. If anything, Valerie came here only out of morbid curiosity."

Metal clanged when Adam dropped the tape measurer and it hit the pipe on the ground. Long strides closed the distance between them in seconds. His hands circled Tesha's waist and he pulled her against him with so much force, she gasped. His hungry mouth fell over hers just as she opened to ask what he planned. Instantly the sparks in her veins traveled to her brain because all she knew was that she had to be with him.

Tesha entwined her arms around his waist and pulled him closer. The hardness of his body melted any resolve that may have existed. God she hoped he never stopped kissing her.

Her lips parted and his tongue filled her mouth and she suckled it, while it tangled with hers. What was it about this man that encompassed all of her being? His touch immediately erased any surroundings, any coherent thought.

Adam slipped his arm under her legs and the other around her waist and lifted her. He carried her to the house. Before she could protest, his lips slid from her mouth to the side of her neck causing scathing sensations so wonderful, her head fell back.

How she needed this, to lose control with him. Truth be told, she'd dreamed and fantasied about Adam every night since meeting him. Her mind filled and went over all sorts of erotic scenes that featured a very naked and yummy Adam Ford.

They made it as far as the screened in porch and fell into a wicker couch where his muscular body fell over hers, the weight of him so incredibly delicious. Tesha ran her fingers through his dark thick hair when he lowered to trace his tongue from her throat to the tops of her breasts. "I—I want you," she stuttered, unable to catch a full breath. "I want you so badly, Adam."

He yanked her dress up and slid her panties down then tossed them onto the floor. She squirmed in anticipation already wet. His eyes traveled to between her legs, and darkened. With his lips parted and chest expanding with his harsh breaths, Adam traced his fingers down her quivering stomach to the precise spot that would be her undoing and stroked her until she came. The eroticism of him watching her dissolve by his touch made her want him even more.

Tesha moaned when he pushed her further until she lifted her hips to meet his movements. "Take your clothes off, Adam." She'd never been demanding when making love, but with Adam she wanted to make sure to get as much from him as he was willing to give.

He straightened and continued to look down at her. Motionless and devoid of expression, his eyes took her in.

Her breathing hitched. For a moment she panicked thinking he was not going to comply. But when his hands reached for the zipper of his pants, she relaxed and watched. Adam never took his gaze from her face as he slid the jeans down his narrow hips. Although she knew he was well built, she was not prepared for the beautiful contours of his muscled thighs. On his left thigh jagged scars marred his otherwise smooth skin. She didn't give the scarring any additional notice. Instead the thick enticing cock that jutted from between his legs riveted her.

The prominence of his arousal took all her attention and she licked her lips. One day she'd have that part of him between her lips. Right now, she needed Adam deep inside her. With quick movements, she grabbed her bunched up sundress and ripped it off over her head. Before she could toss it, Adam was over her, his thick thighs parting her legs.

"Wait." She pushed against his shoulders. "Protection." If he didn't have a condom, Tesha would have to kill something from frustration.

Adam blinked. It took a moment for her words to register though the focus of taking her. "Yeah. Hold on." He dashed from the room and was back sooner than humanly possible.

Tesha was impatient, her gaze following his every move as he tore the wrapping with his teeth and shielded himself. He leaned over her and once again pushed her legs apart to settle between them. His hot mouth covered her right breast and he suckled on her nipple with force. Tesha bucked up into him, but he did not move to enter her.

Not giving him time to be considerate, she reached between them and took his penis directing it to her center. "I need you to take me now. Don't be gentle, I want to feel your strength, your hard body slamming against mine."

He thrust into her with no gentleness and both groaned at the same time.

"Yes!" Tesha grabbed his butt and pulled him further in. "Oh, God."

Adam pulled out almost completely, his arms quivered with the effort and he pushed back inside slamming against her. Again and again, he lunged, his hips lifting high before lowering to drive his length fully in.

Before long Tesha was lost in the abyss of their lovemaking. She shouted out his name while raking her nails down his back as he drove in and out of her in a steady pace.

The room began to spin and she held on to him. No it was too soon Tesha didn't want to come yet. She craved to remain lost in the passion for a while longer. She forced her breathing to slow and opened her eyes to watch Adam.

His eyes were closed; the utter beauty of the man amazed her. His long lashes swept down, contradictory to the tightness of his lips and crinkle of concentration between his brows. The thick cords on his neck and shoulders strained against his smooth sun-kissed skin and rivulets of perspirations trickled from his temples.

Tesha gasped when his eyes opened and pinned hers. The overwhelming emotion emanating from the depths of his blue eyes made it impossible to look away, to tear from the net he cast over her.

Her entire body shook with release and she screamed out, unable to control the tremors that came from where they were joined at her legs. "Oh, God!!" Although lost in the abyss of a myriad of sensations, she felt Adam's thrusts until he too cried out and came with the force of a man long denied.

When he finally stopped shaking, he lowered beside her, pulling Tesha to lie on her side so they could remain joined. She lifted her leg and draped it over his hip. His eyes were closed, his chest heaving. Tesha ran a finger down the center of his pecs. "I wondered how it would be between us. You are amazing."

He looked at her for a moment and then down to her breasts. "We're not done yet."

"Should we worry someone may walk by and see us?" She wiggled her hips and jutted them forward to take him in deeper.

He groaned and pulled her closer against him. "I don't care."

She pressed kisses to his jawline and neck and was pleasantly surprised when his body began to react and he hardened fully once again. "You're beautiful, Adam." She looked up see a lightness she's never seen in his normally emotionless eyes.

"I don't know how I feel about being called pretty." A corner of his lips lifted. "I'm going to need another condom." He pulled out and got up. Once he removed the shield, he came to her and lifted her from the settee. "Let's finish this in my room."

The only other furnished room in the house was his bedroom. Tesha was surprised at the huge ornate four-poster bed. Soft hues of grey on the wall and bedding along with black pillows gave the room a perfect masculine feel. On both sides of the bed was a gunmetal grey painted table, with black a wrought iron base lamp. She didn't want to ruin the moment by asking, but the designer in her would not be stopped when spotting an abstract painting in shades of grey with an angry slash of red across the center over the fireplace. "Who decorated your bedroom?"

"My mother."

Adam's attention would not be distracted. He fell over her

and began to do delicious things with his tongue from one side of her chest to the other. Tesha's eyes rolled back when he traced a hot path with his tongue down to her flat stomach.

"Oh, no you don't." She pushed at his shoulders when he headed further south. "It's my turn to play. Get on your back, Adam."

She was shocked when he obediently did as told and flipped over. His wary gaze however told her she'd better tread carefully.

She'd be careful all right. The gorgeous man had nothing to fear from her. "I'm going to straddle you." Something told her it was best to tell Adam what she intended to do, to keep from surprising him.

His eyes followed her movements as she climbed over him and then ran her hands down his chest. "I could spend hours exploring you." She smiled at his frown of concentration. "For now, I'll settle for licking you from here," Tesha pressed a fingertip to his left nipple, "to there." She shifted her hips rubbing his erection with her inner thighs.

When Adam visibly swallowed and his nostrils flared, it was apparent he was game.

HE COULDN'T TAKE his eyes off Tesha. Her smooth caramel skin glistened in the soft light. It took all his willpower not to reach for her tantalizing pert breasts. They were not overly large, just big enough to fill his palms. Her enticing lips curved, getting his full attention, the throbbing pulse at her throat fast and steady. "I'm going to kiss you now, Adam."

The huskiness of her voice fell over him like soft caresses and his body reacted before she covered his mouth with hers.

The kiss was sweeter than anything he'd ever tasted, soft pressed across his lips and then deepened the kiss, pushing harder, nipping and licking her way back across his mouth.

Adam reached for her hips, but she pushed his hands away. "Uh-huh," she admonished against his mouth.

Ever so slowly, she continued to kiss and lick him from his jawline to the juncture between his neck and shoulder. Adam moaned and clutched the bedding to keep from grabbing the vixen and rolling over her. Instead he concentrated on the feel of her weight across his midsection, of her hands sliding down his chest. Between soft breaths and murmurs, telling him what she would do to him next and her ministrations, Adam wasn't sure he'd make it much longer. Already his cock strained and throbbed, pulsing under her legs.

"Tesha." He clammed up when her tongue darted to his right nipple. Her tongue swirled around it sending a charge down his body. "Oh shit."

She lifted and glanced up at him. "Are you all right?"

"Yeah. I'm trying not to come."

"Oh." Her lips curved into a devilish grin. "I want to make you feel good, Adam."

"It's working." He grunted when she slid down his body and her lips pressed against the sensitive place right below his belly button. "Tesha…."

The feel of her tongue swirling around the head of his erection made his hips lift off the bed of their own accord. Her fingers curled around the base as her mouth took him in and Adam lost any semblance of control surrendering fully to her.

Chapter Eight

TESHA STUDIED ADAM'S face and held back a giggle. It was interesting to find out he was the stereotypical male. Fell asleep after a second bout of sex with barely a mumbled "you can stay the night."

His chest lifted and lowered with each breath and she couldn't help but press a kiss to his pursed lips.

He scrunched his face and continued to sleep with a soft snore. When he smacked his lips and swallowed, Tesha waited for him to wake. He didn't. She wondered what he dreamed of. At least he seemed to be relaxed.

Adam Ford was amazingly gorgeous. His large body shaped like a Greek god's with perfectly sculpted muscles. He was tall, with wide shoulders and a broad chest that tapered to a flat stomach and narrow hips. And, he had a beautiful ass. She thought so before, but now could verify it having seen it.

All right it was enough of this girly crush thing.

Tesha slid from the bed and reached for a t-shirt that hung on the back of a chair. She tiptoed down the hallway to the screened in porch and picked up her discarded dress, panties, and flip-flops.

As she made her way across the grass to her house, she looked up at the star filled sky and gasped. Thousands of stars twinkled in the darkness, some clearer, some larger than others. The moon was bright, lighting the way but she could not stop looking at it and staring. She spread her arms and turned in circles and smiled.

THE NEXT MORNING, the aroma of her ham and cheese biscuits filled the kitchen as Tesha made her way from it to the dining table while sipping her morning cup of Earl Grey. She stopped short at seeing Adam's face in the glass door. With rumpled hair and wearing a white t-shirt, he frowned while waiting for her to open the door. She wanted to throw herself at him, to kiss him until they were both breathless. Of course that would end up in embarrassment if he came to cut things off and reiterate a relationship between them could not be. Tesha swore under her breath. If he said their night together was a big mistake, she'd smack him.

The knot in her stomach lightened when their gazes met and the expression in his blue eyes was warm, not foreboding. She opened the door and pretended nonchalance. "Good morning, neighbor."

Without a word, he walked in and looked at the walls. She studied him, taking in the still wet hair and his broad back. "Looks good."

He was the most interesting, intriguing man.

"Would you like some tea? The biscuits are done." Tesha waited for him to start the "I can't have a relationship line." If he did, she was going to shove him out the door and lock it. But he surprised her and walked into the kitchen. "Sure."

They each ate two biscuits each and drank tea. Tesha decided to show Adam the current work in progress since he remained silent. "Now I'm trying to find a plumber to replace the faucets in the sinks. I'm at a bit of a standstill and have not done anything in the bathrooms upstairs. They may have to knock holes into the walls so it's silly to paint right now. But I have prepped and painted two other bedrooms rooms so far."

Listened and nodded.

"Want to look?"

"Yes."

She walked up the stairs and he followed. "What do you think?" She pointed to the end of the hallway, which widened toward a window on one side. "I turned this into a little reading nook." In the small space she'd placed a bookshelf and filled it with all her books. There were two overstuffed chairs she'd found in a consignment shop in Atlanta, one on both sides of the small window. The sunlight would provide perfect lighting for reading during the day.

She took his hand and went to an open area to the right of the nook. "I'm trying to figure out if I want to turn this into two rooms or keep it one space and make it a large suite. What do you think?"

For a long while he took in the space. "Are you planning to sleep up here?"

"No. I want to stay downstairs and use the upstairs for my guests. If I keep this room as is. Then I will only have three guest rooms."

He went to stand in the middle of it. "If you split it, the rooms will be very small. I think you should leave it."

"That's what I thought." Tesha loved how they thought alike when it came to her house. How easy it was to be with him although he didn't speak much. Still a part of her wondered what brought him over this morning.

"Why did you leave last night?" His solemn expression did not give any hint of his thoughts.

"I wasn't sure you wanted me to spend the night." Tesha maintained her vow to be honest at all times.

"Before I fell asleep I said you could stay."

She closed the distance between him and looked up at him. "Could."

Adam backed just a bit and shoved his hands into his jean pockets. He lifted his shoulders. "Are you angry?"

Tesha chuckled. "Am I that scary? No, I'm not mad. You didn't say you wanted me to stay. Just said *could*, which is not the same."

Once again he only studied her, not saying a word. Would she ever become used to his lack of movement? How quiet he was? The silence as he pondered her words stretched.

"Hello?" Cleve was downstairs. He'd gone to Nashville for several business meetings. She'd forgotten he was stopping by on his way home.

She narrowed her eyes at Adam. "Saved by the bell."

"I wanted you to stay."

"Really?" It was nice to hear him admit to wanting her to remain with him.

Adam neared and leaned in, his eyes locked with hers. Tesha lifted her face wanting to feel his lips on hers. He straightened and took a step backward breaking the spell.

"Hey, there you are," Cleve said from the doorway, his eyes darting from her to Adam. "Hello."

A stiff nod was Adam's only response.

Her friend walked in and looked around the space. "This room is too big." Cleve gave Tesha a puzzled look when she shook her head. "What are you doing with it?"

"I'm going to make it a suite," she replied.

They made their way downstairs back to the kitchen. Adam gave her a long look then excused himself and left. She could tell Cleve waited for her to say something about her neighbor. It was best to let him ask whatever questions he wanted. Tesha served him biscuits and a cup of coffee and sat opposite him at the kitchen table.

"I don't like him," Cleve told her between bites. "He's got a big chip on his shoulder. Not very friendly."

Tesha shrugged. "I suppose he does come across that way. But he's a good guy."

"Is he going to do more work upstairs?" Cleve would not stop asking questions until he felt reassured. "I'm not sure you're safe alone with him. He watches you too much."

"Maybe it's because I'm a hot number," Tesha joked and shimmied her shoulders. She laughed when Cleve gave her a droll look.

"I'm serious. You are a beautiful woman, Tesha. And that's what worries me. He has this propriety air when looking at you and it's almost like he challenges me. Maybe someone should check into his background."

Soft knocks saved her from more of Cleve's comments. Mrs. Miller stood at the door holding a beautiful flowering-hanging basket. Tesha moved back to allow the woman to enter. Mrs. Miller took a deep breath. "Happy housewarming! Oh my, it sure smells delicious."

Cleve went to the lady and relieved her of the basket. "Tesha makes the best ham and cheese biscuits. I can eat a dozen if I'm not careful."

"Mrs. Miller, how nice to see you." Tesha introduced her new visitor to Cleve, who immediately began asking her questions about her store. Cleve had to be the most inquisitive person Tesha ever met.

While her visitors chatted and Mrs. Miller ate a biscuit, Tesha prepared a small basket with several more for the older woman to take to her book club. Although she'd been invited, Tesha didn't feel ready to meet a group of widows at once. Not yet.

"Mrs. Miller," Cleve began, glancing towards Tesha, "the guy next door has been helping Tesha with some construction work in the house. Do you feel he's trustworthy enough to be alone with her?"

"Cleve!" Tesha pictured hitting him upside the head with a hammer.

Mrs. Miller chuckled. "He's a hero. Of course, she's safe. Adam told me the other day about coming here to help you."

Tesha was surprised that Adam would actually hold a conversation with someone. "He did?"

"Yes," Mrs. Miller sipped from her teacup. "He also told me he warned you about his PTSD."

"PTSD?" Cleve shook his head. "I suppose he needs the work. What kind of warning?" He gave Tesha a pointed look.

"Adam told me it's best if he works alone during the day that I not be here with him by myself."

"But you were when I got here." Cleve pointed out the obvious.

"He said if he felt anxiety coming on, he'd tell me and leave."

"You're so naïve. The man barely talks."

If only Cleve knew how well Adam communicated with his body.

Once again Mrs. Miller laughed. "From what I understand, Adam has always been a quiet man. He needs the work because it's best for him to keep busy. Adam Ford doesn't need money."

"He doesn't?" Tesha's mind turned into Cleve mode. "What did he do before joining the service?"

"The Army." Mrs. Miller let out a breath. "Adam was a CEO of Ford Enterprise in Nashville. They are one of the biggest commercial marketing companies in the southeast. He left it all to go to Afghanistan."

"Why?" Both Cleve and Tesha asked in unison.

"His brother told me it was a combination of their younger brother, Caden, joining and wanting to protect him and the loss of a good friend and business partner when the towers fell."

Tesha sank down and picked at a biscuit. "Did Caden…"

"He's fine." Mrs. Miller patted her hand. "He's a police officer in Nashville now."

Cleve remained after Mrs. Miller left. She knew he had something in mind to remain so late when facing a six-hour drive to Atlanta. Tesha sat on the couch while Cleve sat on the other end and flipped through channels. "Go ahead tell me what you're thinking," Tesha told him, not sure she wanted to have the conversation.

"I'm worried about you." He glanced to her and then to the television, which showed a woman pimping an ugly embroidered blouse on a shopping channel. "I think you're ready for a relationship, but just not with that guy."

On one hand she loved Cleve and knew he wanted the best for her, but one of the reasons for moving from Atlanta was to get away from what he and her parents pictured as the type of man she should date.

"Because he's not a preppy executive and member of a tennis club? Cleve, I don't know if I will pursue a relationship with Adam, but if I do, it will be because he is a good man. Who I date will be my choice and I am not going to give a damn whether or not you or anyone agrees with my choices." Tesha was on a roll. "Did I say anything when you dated that skank Melody Poll who was after your money?"

She was gratified by Cleve's embarrassed look. "You got me there. And it has nothing to do with status."

"You keep telling yourself that." Tesha was angry. "My mother never ceased to point out how I could have aspired to marry higher and 'settled' for David. David was a great man, I was privileged he chose to marry me. Look, I know you all want the best for me, but trust me. Please, let me make my own decisions."

"What worries me is his illness, sweetheart." Cleve's eyes met hers. "He may never get better. May not be able to have a normal life. Especially if he's not getting treatment. And if he is getting help, even then there are no guarantees."

After Cleve left, Tesha poured a glass of cabernet and found a jazz station on her phone. She allowed the music and wine to soothe her as she lay on the couch.

He may never get better.

How bad was Adam's PTSD? She had to find out if things ever became more than just physical between them.

Chapter Nine

THE ENGINE RUMBLED to life and Adam felt the vibrations of the '65 Ford Fairlane as it started for the first time in many years.

The smell of engine oil and leather took him back to working in the garage on old cars with his father. For as long as he could remember, he and his brothers would take turns helping while their dad tinkered under the hood of whatever car he worked on that year. Eventually as they grew into teenagers, each of them found a car and he'd help them fix it to drive. It was second nature to Adam to spend time working on old cars.

He climbed out of the car to check under the hood. All seemed to be working well. It was ready for a test drive. Months spent restoring the car and finally he was almost done. All it needed was a tank full of gas and final adjustments to the idle.

That morning the last part arrived. He'd hurried out to the garage barely able to sustain the excitement. It was satisfying to hear the engine's first roar. Vince would be so proud.

He'd done it, completed two of the projects his friend spoke of nonstop the entire time they'd been stationed together in Afghanistan.

Vince Bailey's conversations had revolved around three

subjects, the house, the car, and his future wife. Vince hadn't met the woman he planned to marry, but that never stopped him from talking about her as if she already existed.

Give me three. Three years, Ford, and you'll see. I'll have the trifecta. A sexy car to get the smokin' hot girl. The amazing house that will make her fall in love with me and then a sexy wife to be with me for the rest of my life. You'll see, Ford. When you come over for barbeques.

He'd laugh when Adam rolled his eyes. An infectious laughter that made others join in.

It was too quiet in the garage after he cut off the engine. Adam walked around the car, inspecting every single detail.

The black glossy paint set off the bright red interior with white piping. Just like Vince had described. When it came to the house Adam had been more at liberty since his friend did not go to as much detail. But at the hospital, Vince had gone over every detail of how he planned to fix up the car. It must have been his way of dealing with the pain of so many wounds.

Adam would take the car for a trial drive, and then it was time to make the phone call.

Two days later

VINCENT BAILEY SR. wiped his eyes while walking around the car. "You did it, son." His moist eyes met Adams. "You restored it exactly like Vince would have."

Adam remained quiet, allowing the older man, whose striking resemblance to his friend always took him by surprise, to talk.

"I bet Vince's up there grinning ear to ear." Vince's father took out his handkerchief and blew his nose. "Can I drive it?"

"It's yours."

The man shook his head. "Vince told me clearly. The car and house were to be yours." He lifted his hand to silence Adam when he went to speak. "He got his love of cars from me. I have five in my garage and house, right now. Last thing I need is another one, my wife already grumbles nonstop saying I need to sell a couple. Besides it'll help with the third part of the plan." He grinned and years melted of his face. "Don't give me that look. I bet you already got your eye on a girl. Come on, let's cruise."

They rode for miles without a destination. Mr. Bailey lowered the volume on the radio. He kept his eyes on the long patch of country road and spoke. "So it seems to me like you got the house and the car, now all you need is the wife. What you doing about it?"

Adam watched the passing scenery. Even after living in the state most of his life, he never tired of it. Tennessee was beautiful. "I'm trying my best, Mr. Bailey." It was a lie, but the last thing he needed was someone else badgering him about getting married.

"If anyone deserves a good life, it's you. After what you did, saving all those boys' lives over there."

"Didn't save Vince."

"You got him out of there. He lived long enough for us to say goodbye." The older man's voice cracked on the last word, and they rode in silence a bit longer. "That is worth more than gold to me."

Lazy cows grazed in the distance and Adam wondered what life would be like for him if he could have it all, the pie in the sky as it were.

As if reading his thoughts Vincent Bailey broke the silence. "Vince told me you were married once already and that she left you. He hoped you'd find someone better. He would have been married by now I'm sure. That boy did most things he set his mind to."

"I can't."

"Son, you have to leave it behind. If you don't, it'll eat you up inside. Don't let it. Get some help. It won't go away on its own. You should know that by now."

Adam nodded, only to make Mr. Bailey feel better. He didn't have any intention of seeking counseling. He'd done plenty of research, only a scant few who had it as bad as he did, made it through and were able to have normal lives. It was either that or they were walking time bombs. Personally, he didn't believe it was ever possible to get rid of the violence trapped inside his mind.

"You'll never know if you don't try. Broken people are like broken clay pots. They can be put back together. I know it will never be the same when the pieces are glued. There will be cracks. But those cracks, they add personality. Tell a story of survival. Of strength, of character."

Adam remained silent. Mr. Bailey turned the knob and a country song came on. Tim McGraw sang about making the most out of life and Mr. Bailey gave Adam a triumphant look. "See there, Vince agrees with me. Sent that song." He hummed along to the music as they headed back.

An hour later when Adam went to close the garage door, a pair of dog tags hanging from the rear-view mirror caught his attention. Mr. Bailey must have left them.

Vinnie's last words were as clear as if his friend spoke them out loud.

Live a good life, Adam. You better make it a good one 'cause you're gonna be living mine, too.

Rapid chopping sounds of the helicopters blades and the sounds of his heart beating hard did not stop that night while Adam pushed up and down from the floor, exercising until his arms trembled and gave out and he collapsed onto the wooden floor. He rolled to his back and began doing sit-ups.

His eyes searched in vain past the gruesome pictures that flashed around him. A familiar item, some sort of focal point to distract him from the horrible images would help. His stomach cramped in protest and he fell back gasping. The neon numbers from the clock on the nightstand glowed casting an eerie glow across the floor where he lay. It was three-thirty in the morning.

A few moments later, wearing a hooded sweatshirt, he ran from the house. Perhaps a few miles of running would exhaust him enough to fall into a dreamless slumber.

A light flickered outside Tesha's house. He made a wide circle on the road to jog past.

Barefoot, in her short nightshirt, she paced inside with a glass of wine in her hand. She seemed to be swaying to music. When she wiped a tear from her cheek, the action tore into Adam's chest. He wanted nothing more than to go to her, to comfort her from whatever it was that kept her awake.

Chop. Chop. Chop. Chop.

The sounds of the helicopter blades returned and he turned running as fast as he could away from her.

Two broken souls, he and Tesha were. It was probably what brought them together. Like calls to like, and all that. No, it was more than that. She called to him in a way that had nothing to do with her brokenness. Yes, her husband was dead, a victim of the same war, but she'd moved on. Unlike him, she didn't have the anxiety of having experienced all the death and violence. Instead of allowing the past to claim her, she moved forward. Helped others, smiled, and gave. The woman impressed him to no end.

He thought back to her in his bed, straddling him. Her beautiful naked body over his, the plush curves he'd ran his hands over. Tesha made love to him like no one else had. Her lips on his skin were like a soothing balm to his tortured soul.

Lightness lifted in his chest with such swiftness he stopped running and stood in the middle of the isolated road. Overhead the stars glistened and for the first time in hours, when he removed the headphones all he heard were the songs of crickets. He waited and listened.

Adam turned and sprinted back. He went to her back door and she opened it. "Adam?"

He went to her and pulled her against him, instantly his mouth over hers in an attempt to take all her worries away, to soothe her like she'd done him. Tesha reacted by wrapping her arms around his neck and moaning softly.

His mission became to replace the saltiness of her tears with the taste of their kisses. "I want to make love to you. Help you forget."

With sudden strength, she pushed him away her eyes lifting to him. For a few beats her eyes searched his face. "I don't want to forget anything, Adam. I am being silly. Mad because I couldn't sleep and my first reaction was to go to your house. To go to you. I'm all right." She reached and cupped his face. "Especially now that you came to me instead."

Sliding his arm under her legs, he lifted her and carried her to the bedroom. He kissed her temple. "I'm a sweaty mess. Want to take a shower together?"

"Yes."

THE SUN WAS high in the horizon by the time Adam walked into his house.

In the kitchen his brother Jensen looked up and instantly tried to hide the worried look. "Hey, bro. You're out and about early."

"Went for a run."

"Long run."

Adam ignored him and went to the coffee pot. Jensen had already made coffee. With a fresh beverage in hand, he sat on a barstool and watched as his brother attempted to make pancakes. All of his brothers could cook. Besides spending time in the garage with their father, they all shared the cooking duties with their mom. She'd taught them each not just the basics, but also a special recipe. His was lasagna, Jensen's was definitely not pancakes. The ones he'd already made were odd shaped and lumpy.

"Hungry?" His brother said over his shoulder.

"Yep."

They ate in companionable silence. Jensen checked his

email on an open laptop while eating the amazingly good pancakes.

He looked up from the screen. "I got a movie coming up and they want to shoot in a small town. I suggested Lovely. This house."

Adam groaned. Jensen was the hottest movie star in Hollywood so his suggestions were taken seriously. Being voted sexiest man alive didn't stop him from being the pesky younger brother to Adam.

"No way. They already treat me like I'm some big shot in this town. Don't need you prancing around town making it worse."

"You are a big shot. An all-American hero. The best kind."

"Pick a different town."

Jensen gave him the "it's too late" look and Adam hung his head. "When?"

"A couple weeks, or a month. You know how it is, nothings ever on schedule." His brother became animated. One thing he could say for Jensen, the guy genuinely loved what he did. "I'm going to play an immortal hero with super powers, who goes to a small town to attempt a normal life."

Adam continued to eat and Jensen reached over and jabbed at his shoulder. "Aren't you interested in what my super powers will be?"

"Muteness?"

"Nah. I'm going to have the ability to read minds and I'll have an awesome metal arm."

"Cool."

"Yeah."

"You're not doing it here."

"Can't change it, I don't have any control over it."

"Damn it, Jensen."

His brother gave him his usual crooked smile that women went crazy over. Adam, not so much. He wanted to punch him in the face at the moment. "Hey, if you're nice to me, I'll get you a walk-on part."

"That's so not happening."

Chapter Ten

"YOU SHOULD GO see about him." Mrs. Miller watched Tesha closely. She'd been looking out the window towards Adam's house. It had been several days since she'd seen him. The morning after they'd made love, he'd been gone when she woke. Tesha did not want to go after him, especially if he needed space and privacy. They did not have the type of relationship where she felt comfortable enough to go to his home and ask what happened.

For a couple of days, there had been a car in Adam's driveway, a sleek classic black Jaguar. One morning, Tesha caught sight of a man walking around the car, talking into a cell phone, but she couldn't make out his features. She suspected it was one of Adam's three brothers, by the resemblance in height and build.

"He warned me that if he ever stayed away it was best for me not to go after him. My guess is, he's afraid to hurt me if he's having an episode. Besides, I don't want to be the nosy neighbor." She flushed and attempted to hide behind her teacup. "He had a visitor. Looked like one of his brothers."

Mrs. Miller smiled into her cup of tea. "You're more than neighbors. When he mentioned you, his face softened. I think he's sweet on you and you are not indifferent to him either, are you?"

How insightful this woman was. Tesha shook her head and couldn't help another glance out the window. "No, Mrs. Miller I am not indifferent to Adam Ford, but I am smart enough to know it's best to not get too attached to a man like him."

"Love conquers many things." By her friend's faraway look it was obvious she no longer saw the immediate surroundings. "I haven't told you how I came to end up here in Lovely."

Mrs. Miller's smile became soft. "I was so in love with Randy Miller that I could barely stand it. He was handsome and best of all, in spite of being quite popular in our town, set his eyes on me. When he was drafted to go to Vietnam in 1970, he asked me to marry him. How I wish I would have." She let out a sigh.

"But my parents didn't care for the fast boy, as they called him and I wasn't brave enough to stand up to them. So he left and I cried myself to sleep for many nights." She took a sip of her tea and look out the window to Adam's house.

"Adam reminds me of him in a way. We wrote, Randy and I for months, and then suddenly his letters stopped. I was terrified that he may have been killed, so I went to his house. The entire family was gone. I was told his father was in jail and his mother had moved south to Florida."

Mrs. Miller's eyes welled. "It took me a long time to get over him. I hated myself for not marrying Randy when he'd asked me. Eventually I got married to Edward, a boy my parents approved of. Bless his heart, the dullest man I've ever known. The most exciting thing Edward did was mow the grass." They chuckled together.

"So," Mrs. Miller continued. "After Edward died in his forties suddenly of a heart attack. God knows how that happened, but that's not a nice thing to say, I decided to return to Tennessee and start anew. Not sure where to exactly settle, I read a magazine article about a small town that was restoring itself. I opened the pages, and there in front of Miller's hardware stood Randy Miller."

"Oh my goodness. What did you do?" Tesha exclaimed barely able to sit still.

Mrs. Miller laughed at her excitement. "I raced here as fast as my old car would take me. I hadn't seen Randy in twenty years, but as soon as I walked into the store, he ran to me and we hugged. We got married two weeks later."

"That is so romantic." Tesha sniffed. "I hate that you lost him again so soon after."

"Yes," Mrs. Miller replied with another deep sigh. "Randy died in a car accident. A woman hit him while searching in her purse for something."

"That's horrible."

"We had twenty-five wonderful years."

Tesha reached for Mrs. Miller's hand. "I only had five years with David."

The women remained silent for a long time, each lost in the memories of having found love and the great pain that came with that loss.

AFTER MRS. MILLER left, Tesha walked around her house with a clipboard making notes to update her project board. If all went well, she would be open for business in two months' time. First she'd have to come up with a name and set up her business license. Besides painting and finishing her garden space, the plumbing and wiring had to be completed.

"Now to find a good name." She wrote down "The Haven" on her piece of paper. Then scratched it out. Did the same with several more ideas. Nothing struck a chord. Finally, she sat on the stairs and closed her eyes. The house had a certain feel to it, a restlessness about it that was interesting. Almost as if it too could not wait to fulfill its purpose. She inhaled deeply and listened. Soft jazz music from her office filled the air, a hint of rosemary from the plant outside the kitchen window tickled her nose, and then she sensed it. Peace. The elusive thing she'd been waiting for. The breeze caressed her face as if reaching to her and soothing her soul.

This house would disclose its name when it was ready and it would be the perfect place for war widows to come and be alone, away from the pitying glances and the day-to-day demands. For one week, they'd do nothing more than read, garden, drink tea, and rest. Tesha's lips curved. It would be the place she wished she could've escaped to when David died.

The knock on the door startled her. Adam was on the other side of the glass holding a baking dish. From his arm a plastic bag dangled. Tesha's stomach pitched at his handsome face. The affect he had on her was both troublesome and exciting.

His face remained impassive when she opened the door.
She smiled up at him. "Hi."
"I brought dinner."
"That's great." Her stomach grumbled at the wonderful smell. "Did you make me your famous lasagna?"
He nodded. "I brought some bread and two bottles of wine too. I wasn't sure what kind you'd like."
Tesha moved back to let him pass and took the bag from

his arm once he placed the pan of lasagna on the counter. He watched in silence as she removed the cork on the bottle of merlot and poured two glasses. Self conscious at his scrutiny, Tesha held a glass out to him. "How have you been?"

He shrugged instead of replying. "Where are your plates?"

"Here," Tesha told him while attempting to gauge his mood and opened a cabinet and took two plates out. Then put them on the counter.

Adams arms went around her from behind and he kissed her shoulder. "I've been thinking about you."

His mouth covered hers when she turned to look at him. The kiss was perfect, what she'd been missing and it ended too soon when her stomach grumbled. "Let's get you fed." Adam reached for the spatula.

While Adam cut the pasta and placed it on the plates, Tesha set the table for two. She wanted to tell him so many things. Ask him about the past days, what he'd done and why he'd not called or come by. But she supposed he could say the same in response. But she'd been told to stay away and damn it, she'd not make a fool of herself by chasing after him.

His eyes met hers when they sat on the table and began eating. "I hope you like it."

Everything became him at once. All she could taste, see, hear, and sense was Adam. Her entire being submersed in him, as if dunked under water and not able to feel anything other than the water. She inhaled sharply and swallowed. How had it come to this? What did he do to her that could affect her so much?

She wanted a relationship, yes, but only a casual one at this point. This felt like so much more and it terrified her. Perhaps it happened to everyone with someone as attractive as Adam was. A relationship with a forbidden person who overwhelms because it's the one nobody wants to find themselves in.

Adam was the first man she'd allowed into her heart since David and it wasn't safe to think it could be something permanent. Tesha lifted the forkful of lasagna to her mouth and ate it. It was amazing. He'd combined herbs into the sauce and the meat so each bite was savory, but not overly seasoned. She met his questioning gaze. "This is delicious. No wonder your mother asks for it."

His lips twitched, the closest she'd seen to him smile. "Thanks."

It was almost sundown, the dimming sunlight streamed into the kitchen, giving it almost a candlelight affect.

Both she and Adam ate a second helping of the pasta dish while she made small talk about the weather and her plans for the garden. Tesha couldn't contain her questions any longer, plus the silence between them when she didn't initiate a topic, stretched longer and gave her too much time to dwell on his effect on her. "I saw a black Jaguar at your house, looked like an expensive, fast car."

His eyes met hers and he nodded. "One of my brothers came for a couple days."

"Was it a good visit?"

"Most of the time, they use any excuse to stop by. To check up on me. So I don't know if this was a legitimate stopover. He claims his work will bring him back for an extended time."

"So it's not just me you keep at arm's length?" She kept her eyes on the wine glass in her hand, nervous she'd overstepped.

"It's best that way."

"What about treatment? Have you looked into it?" This time when she looked at him, he'd sat back in the chair. From his rigid posture, she could tell he wasn't happy at the topic.

"It doesn't work. I'd rather take care of it myself." His closed off expression warned her to back off. Her heart ached for him, knowing that in all this time nothing had worked, or else, he'd not sought help. Her money was on the latter.

"Adam, do you plan to start off all your future relationships with a warning? Is that what you want for your life?"

He drank the rest of the wine in his glass and reached for the bottle. After he refilled hers, he poured a liberal amount into his glass. "I've done the research. Most people don't get better. I've decided not to go to a place and sit in a circle listening to every other crazy person like me talk about their issues."

"If you haven't gone, how do you know what happens? I'm sure every place is different. They structure the therapy according to…"

He stood and picked up their plates, in an obvious attempt to end the direction of the conversation. Tesha's heart went out to him as she watched his tense shoulders while he rinsed the plates. She came up beside him with the pan and split the leftovers into two containers. "I'm keeping some for tomorrow. You can take the rest with you."

They finished cleaning and she refilled their wine glasses, watching him as he read over her business plan notes she'd left on the counter. "You're planning to keep this house a business permanently?"

"No." She shook her head. "After a couple years, I think I would like to make it my home. Maybe by then I'll be ready to get remarried and have a family." She pushed away the picture of him as her husband. "Maybe I'll start with a dog. Speaking of which, what are you building the pen in the back for?

"A dog. One of my buddies is giving me a pup." He didn't elaborate, but she concluded it was someone who he'd served with.

"What kind of dog?"

"German Shepard, I think."

Her lips curved. "And he's going to be an outside dog then?"

"Probably."

"Good luck with that." She smiled and circled her arms around his waist. "Adam, I missed you."

He pulled her closer and placed his chin on top of her head. They remained locked in each other's arms for a while until he moved back. "I better go."

"Hey." Tesha took his arm. "Don't be angry about what I said. I just want you to think about giving yourself a chance for a better life. Yes, it may not work. But it might. You'll never know unless you try."

"I have been thinking about it. Mom gave me some stuff to look over."

He allowed her to pull him down for a kiss. She slipped her fingers from the side of his face through his hair. "Don't leave. Spend the night."

THE NEXT MORNING Tesha stretched relishing the tightness of her body after a night of making love. Adam was everything she could ask for in a lover. In bed he had no trouble communicating. Their bodies were in sync every single second.

He'd left just before dawn and she missed him already.

"Oh no." She pulled the pillow over her face when the sputtering of Fred Shanty's truck sounded in the driveway. He claimed to be a licensed plumber and electrician as well as carpenter and since he'd done a great job on the wall construction, before and after his illness, she decided to give him the work.

If only the man didn't show up so darn early.

Chapter Eleven

THE HOUSE WAS too quiet. Adam turned on the radio in the kitchen and stood in the center of the room waiting. The humming in his ears seemed to dull some and he let out a breath of relief. That morning he'd woken soaked in sweat, his heart thundering against his breastbone. It was almost noon and he'd finally gotten to the point where he could stand still.

He decided it was best to get out of the house, and since he was exhausted from exercising, he drove to town. With the windows down and the just-cool-enough breeze, Adam relaxed.

The bell over the door jingled when he entered the Miller's hardware store.

"Hello, Adam," Mrs. Miller called out to him from somewhere in the back.

Adam went to where pet supplies were kept, he stood in front of the shelves trying to figure out what to get. He'd put off long enough getting the dog, and decided the coming weekend would be a good time to get him.

"Getting a dog?" Mrs. Miller appeared next to him, her face brightened by a smile.

"Yes, ma'am."

"Well, you need to be prepared. Let's get to work. First you need feeding bowls, a crate…" As she rattled off her list, she pulled items from the shelf for his inspection.

Before long he loaded his truck with all the dog supplies. Mrs. Miller walked out behind him with two gallons of paint. "Can you drop these off to Tesha for me? I promised to stop by, but had to cancel. My sister is in the hospital in Michigan, I'm flying out in the morning."

"I will take care of it," Adam told her although he was not quite sure he was up to it today. "Hope your sister is all right."

Mrs. Miller chuckled. "It's nothing too serious. I'm more worried about the store and my replacement here. Jerry Pike is filling in for me. Bless his soul, every time he does, he loses things or falls asleep and spends the night behind the counter."

The drive home was shaping up to be as relaxing as the drive in and Adam hoped it meant his evening would be without incident. Something rolled into the road and he stopped breathing. He jerked the wheel to the left and the truck swerved, tires screeching. Brightness filled his vision and he pushed down on the brakes while maneuvering the truck toward the edge of the road. His hands shook on the steering wheel. When he held them up, blood dripped from them. So much blood. Someone screamed and he jumped at the sound. He fought with the door handle and jumped from the truck to find himself standing in a dirt road he didn't remember turning off on. The only thing in the middle of the road was a dried bush the wind had blown over.

He stumbled to the side of the truck and fell against it squeezing his eyes shut. This sucked. Not knowing when the damn flashbacks would occur was the worst. Adam lifted his hands and they were clean. No blood.

Once he arrived at his house, he took his time unloading

his purchases. It didn't take too long to set everything up in the screened in porch. It was time to deliver Tesha's paint.

Cars drove by and circled. It seemed Aaron Moore was having one of his social events by the three cars already parked along the road. He remembered receiving an invitation for something from the neighbor who he'd only spoken to a few times. Adam wondered absently if Tesha would go to the gathering. If she'd already left, he could just leave the paint and not have to face her. He was on shaky ground; it was best to keep a safe distance tonight.

Besides, once he saw her, he'd have to tell her they'd not be seeing each other any longer.

On the way home from town, he'd made the decision to cut things off between them, it was best not to speak to her until he could handle things better. As insightful as she was, once he faced her, she'd immediately know things had changed between them.

Unfortunately, she was home and looked gorgeous and immediately all his resolve flew out the window. He could barely swallow at seeing her in a calf length sleeveless dress. It was a bright green with small black flowers along the bottom and under her breasts. In her hair, she'd pinned a cloth flower in the same green hue. Her lips glistened with some sort of lip color when she smiled up at him. "Hello, Adam."

Her eyes were warm at meeting his and it took all he had to keep from blurting out he didn't want her to go to the neighbor's house. What if another man saw her, took her from him. Damn he was a confused fool.

"You can just put those inside the door," Tesha moved back and went to the kitchen counter where she'd left a glass of wine. "Would you like some wine?"

"Are you going to Moore's party?"

She frowned and studied his attire. "I take it you're not. Yes, I'm going. It's my chance to see the interior of that house." She cocked her head to the side. "Why don't you come with me?"

It was so tempting, especially when she placed the glass down and walked away to peer out the front window. Her pert butt filled out the dress perfectly and he wanted nothing more at the moment than to grab it as he pumped into her.

Tesha gasped when he took her arm and swirled her to face him. His mouth crashed onto hers and he pulled her against him with enough force she would not have any doubt how much he wanted her.

Every curve of her called to him. It was as if he'd not known another woman. As if her fresh smell, the taste of her lips, every inch of her silken skin was made especially for him. Although he'd have a hard time describing what he felt for her, it would rank past lust, although desire was definitely a part of it.

She wiggled in his arms, her hands pushing against his chest. But he couldn't stop, had to have her. His smell would be on her when she went to that party. There would be no question she was another's. He yanked her dress up.

"Adam, stop." Her words penetrated the fog, just enough to make him wonder what they meant. "You're scaring me." She attempted to shove him away.

Every movement she made drew him to want her more, to take her over and over until she could say nothing more than his name. Tesha had become something important to him. He was in love with her and fought to tell her through his kisses, and touches what couldn't be spoken out loud.

The slap echoed in his ears.

It was a second or two before he realized Tesha had struck him. She scurried away from him, to stand beside the door and yanked it open.

"What is wrong with you? You were scaring me." It was then he noticed the tears. Her face was pale, eyes wide. "Leave." Her bottom lip trembled.

"I'm sorry." Adam could not look at her. He moved closer and she leaned away. "Let me explain." He couldn't end things like this. Not by scaring her.

"Get out!" She pulled the door open wider and held it. "We can talk later, but not now. I don't know what's come over you, but I need you to leave."

Minutes later he stumbled into his house and picked up the closest object, a plate. The dish exploded into thousands of pieces when he threw it against the wall. "I hate this." He growled in frustration and stalked from one side of the room to the other. "I can't be with Tesha, can't be with anyone. I hate it!" No matter how calm of an existence he tried to lead, how much he exhausted his body with fruitless activity, the result was always the same. His disorder robbed him of any kind of normal.

The knock on the door made him jump. He hoped it was Tesha and he could apologize for his actions.

He opened the door and found her standing on the porch, her arms tight across her chest. "Are you okay?"

He shook his head and looked down to the floor. "I don't know. Please forgive me."

How he wanted her to come inside and sit down, talk with him and give him a chance to tell her how badly he wanted normalcy. Convince her to forgive him. God how he wished it was possible to be in a true relationship with her.

She didn't move and he didn't invite her to enter. He was too unstable, feared he'd lose it again.

"I am not mad at you, Adam. What I am is concerned."

Adam nodded, and closed his eyes. When he opened them, she was gone.

Night came and he peered out the windows toward Moore's house. The party seemed to be in full swing. Several people lingered on the porch, cocktails in hand. It had been his life once. He'd thrown cocktail parties in his house near Nashville for clients and employees.

Now it seemed like someone else's life, a faraway part of himself he'd never see again. He looked back over his shoulder. The brochure on the kitchen counter caught his attention. In two days, his mother expected him to join her at the clinic. Instead he planned to go pick up the dog.

Adam found himself on the front porch. It was a warm night, soft music and the sounds of laughter traveled from the party. He narrowed his eyes when several women walked outside. It was not Tesha. At her house only the downstairs lights were on, which was normal. He had no way of knowing if she'd gone to the party or been too upset after what he'd done to go.

Jealousy. The feeling had taken him by surprise and he'd reacted in a horrible way. He'd never been the type to not trust someone, to feel that another could take a woman's attentions from him. Of course, he'd never been broken before either.

Since returning from the war, he'd been with a few women. Mostly one-night stands he'd met while in Nashville. Women who'd not tempted him to more than one tryst.

In Lovely, he'd considered beginning a relationship. Getting to know someone. Yes, he'd planned to several times, had gone as far as to buy condoms, but when the time came to ask a woman to go out with him, he'd not been able to. Tesha was the first woman he allowed close. He regretted it now. Mainly because of the pain he already felt at losing her.

And lose her he would.

The phone rang. Jensen again.

Chapter Twelve

TESHA COULDN'T SHAKE the feeling something was horribly wrong. The look in Adam's eyes, as if he struggled to remain in control shook her. What would it take to get him help? Obviously his family was trying, they gave him brochures and checked in on him. They'd probably spoken to Adam many times and tried to convince him to get help.

What needed to be done was to not give him a choice. Someone going through so much could not make a wise decision. At this point, it was unlikely Adam was able to understand what was best.

The best thing for her at the moment was a distraction. She went to the bathroom and to touch up her make up. Her reflection made her hesitate. Wide eyes looked back at her and her lipstick was smeared. Letting out a deep breath, she repaired it.

THE AIR WAS brisk as she made her way around to the wraparound porch of Moore's house. It was a beautiful house inside and out. The details of every space in the house were done with care and knowledge. Through the window the voices of people carried along with the music and she drank her glass of wine content for the moment.

It was such a different life from the hustle and bustle of

Atlanta. She missed her friends and the convenience of large chain stores. But Nashville was only an hour away and everything she needed right now was here in Lovely. Fireflies danced in the air and she couldn't take her eyes from them. It had been years since she'd seen them.

They flew in the direction of Adam's house. Through the living room window she saw his lights flickered then went out. Something happened. Not stopping to think, she placed her glass on the railing and rushed over to check.

She stood on the porch and put her ear to the door. Adam's house was quiet. She wasn't sure whether to knock or just walk in. "Oh for goodness sakes. You've seen the man naked, why not walk in." Tesha mumbled and she opened the door. "Adam?"

A groan sounded and she went toward his bedroom. "What's wrong?"

He was on the floor, kneeling beside his bed. His right knuckles were bruised and bloody, probably from hitting something. She looked to the wall beside the door. Holes were punched into the drywall. Tesha hesitated, not sure what to do.

"Please, go home, Tesha." He sounded tired, defeated. "I'm a lost cause."

"No, you're not." Tesha went to the bathroom and ran a washcloth under the water. She neared slowly and wrapped his hand with it. "You're a good man, Adam."

He chuckled, but it was not with mirth. "That's right, I'm a fucking hero." He move away and stood. "I keep forgetting. I'm a goddamned hero."

"I'm going to get you some water."

"No." His entire body trembled.

She wondered if it was because he held back. Tesha ignored the shiver of apprehension. Adam wouldn't really hurt her. "Tell me what I can do to help you."

It was heartbreaking to see the proud, beautiful man slump. "Help me by forgetting I exist. Don't let me near you again." He swallowed visibly. The pain in his eyes was piercing when he looked at her. "You deserve so much better than me. I can barely make it day-to-day, Tesha. Stop wasting your time with me."

"I want to help you," she whispered, not wanting to give up. Couldn't he see, it was too late? She was already in love with him. Needed him like she needed air. Wanted no one but him.

"That's the thing." He walked to the window and looked outside. "I don't want your help. I don't want anyone's help. I'm sick and tired of everyone offering to help. I want to be left the fuck alone."

"Why?" Tesha wanted to push the soft locks that fell over his brow and kiss the pain away. "Tell me, Adam, why do you want to be alone?"

A single tear slid down from the corner of his eye, it trailed to his jaw and splashed onto his shirt. "I can't talk anymore. Please leave."

The crickets' songs from outside were the only sound in the room. Tesha wasn't sure what else could be said. If Adam refused help, didn't want to try, there was little she could do. It certainly was beyond her capabilities to help him.

"The war killed David, my husband. The vehicle he was in ran over an IED. He didn't have a choice. You on the other hand, have a choice, yet you allow the war to take your life, too." She could not keep the tears from falling when he didn't react. "Fine, Adam. Give up. Some hero you are."

When she reached the front room, she heard him scream, followed by a loud thud against the wall. A loud crash was next followed by an inhuman groan.

He was losing it. A cell phone on the counter got her attention. Through the tears and fear of what Adam could be doing, she blindly pushed the buttons.

The screams and thuds continued. While she waited, she'd almost dialed the local sheriff twice. Finally, a bit over an hour later, Tesha stood outside on the porch when the black Lexus SUV pulled up. Three men jumped from the car and rushed to where she stood. She barely had time to register the replicas of Adam, who got out of the vehicle.

Her jaw fell open. Jensen Ford, the movie star, stood in front of her. "Thank you for calling about my brother. This is it. No more talking. We've had enough. It's time for Adam to get help."

She could only nod when the other two neared. The next brother was taller than the others, he moved with smooth grace and elegance. That and the tailor made suit, told of his affluence. The last one was almost identical to Adam. His hair was cropped military short, his eyes held a wariness that reminded her of Adams. Jensen must have known she recognized him, as he didn't introduce himself. "The guy in the suit is our oldest brother, Tristan and the mini Adam, is Caden." Both men were already moving inside.

Tristan stopped before entering. "Thank you for calling Jensen. We appreciate it."

Tesha nodded, her eyes already welling with tears. "Just please help him."

They went inside leaving the door ajar.

She wasn't sure what to do, part of her wanted to run home, while the other needed to be there for Adam. But it was a family situation. No matter what she felt for Adam, it did not give her the right to pry into what would happen between him and his brothers.

Adam cursed and screamed at his brothers to leave. Tesha reached for the wall beside the doorway and leaned on it. Her legs threatened to give out. After a few minutes of the brother's shouting, she moved away and paced up and down the driveway. She kept vigil, not daring go inside her house. Not yet. A few minutes later, she went to her side yard and sunk onto the bench with her arms crossed for warmth.

"Hello?" Jensen walked through the opening where her garden gate would be and came to her. Even in the dimness she could make out his handsome features. He was a bit shorter than Adam, and slimmer than he appeared on the big screen. But the brothers resembled in the broadness of shoulders and muscular physique. He didn't look anything like the cocky actor she'd caught glimpses of on television, instead vulnerability was the only thing she could see in his eyes.

Tesha stood and rubbed her hands down her arms feeling suddenly chilled. "I'm here. Is there anything I can do?"

"Can you keep an eye on my brother's place?" He held out a key ring and a card. "Here's my card. But if anything comes up, please call the number on the back, it's Caden's, he lives closer, in Nashville. He's a cop so he can handle any trouble."

"Of course. But this is a quiet town, I'm sure everything

will be all right. Don't worry." Tesha touched his forearm. "Can I call to ask how he's doing?"

The actor's face softened and he exhaled. "Yeah, of course. I'm sure he'll appreciate it. I better go help." He jogged away and Tesha followed him as far as the front yard.

A few minutes later, the brothers exited, with them a struggling Adam. He was in a rage and didn't seem to notice her. His hair was plastered to his head with sweat as he tried to punch and kick free of their hold. Caden and Tristan held his arms while Jensen had the unfortunate task of holding his feet. It took some work and a lot of cussing by all three, but they finally managed to shove Adam into the SUV and drove off.

THE BEDROOM'S ONLY light came from the moon, the tree outside cast shadows that moved over Tesha's bed. What was happening? Where were they taking Adam? If only she'd asked Jensen more questions.

When the tears flowed, she couldn't stop them, then hiccups followed and she got up and found a box of tissues and brought it to the nightstand. It struck her that grief often came without warning. How could it be that after so long on her own, the man she decided to date was tormented by the same war that killed her husband? If only she'd maintained more of a distance, not allowed Adam close. Now her heart was breaking all over again, not just for herself, but for how much Adam was hurting.

Tesha prayed that he'd do well in whatever treatment his brothers found for him. Now knowing his brother was a movie star, she expected Adam would receive the best treatment since cost would not be much of a hindrance.

MORNING CAME WITH startling brightness. Tesha lay in bed and studied the room. The tall windows were dressed with long sheers of the palest yellow that draped onto the floor. She'd kept the Victorian look with soft floral wallpaper printed with bouquets of yellow and pink rosettes. Her dressing table was a distressed white sideboard cabinet, which she'd shortened the legs on and repainted herself.

The headboard was an intricate iron piece she'd found outside the house. At first she considered using it for the garden gate, but after cleaning it, decided to move it inside. Now refurbished and painted in flat black, it contrasted with the soft colors in the rest of the room in a way that made the bed the focal point of her bedroom. The bedding was all done in buttery yellows and off-white lace trimmed throw pillows.

Tesha stretched and her hand touched something cool. She'd slept with Adam's key ring. The heavy metal with nothing but three keys on it was large hanging from her slim fingers. One was a house key, the second probably for the shed in the back. The third was a car key. She'd not noticed a car other than the truck.

She trudged into the bathroom and caught sight of her reddened eyes in the mirror. The last weeks she'd been so involved in the house and Adam, she'd allowed time to go by without her usual bevy of hair and nail appointments. Her hair had grown a bit longer and barely resembled the pixie cut she normally wore. It was time to either find a beautician in Nashville, or travel back to Atlanta to her usual hairdresser.

She studied herself, for some reason expected to look different. Her eyes were still a light brown; her dark coffee colored hair, although tussled fell just past her chin in the front and shorter in the back. Her eyes traced her body, she'd not gained weight, although her arms were more defined from the physical work.

Again, she studied her face. Other than her swollen eyes, no changes, everything exactly the same in spite of a new heartache.

Mr. Shanty and Jerry Pike did not come to work that day. It was Saturday and she insisted they not work on the weekends anymore. The job was almost done, most of the plumbing and wiring completed for the second floor. She suspected the men didn't mind spending time at her house because of her biscuits and the fact they didn't have a follow-on job. Mr. Shanty offered to help her with painting after the wall patching was complete and she considered it. Perhaps she'd come up with another job for them, they were nice to have around. The exterior of the house was done, the front steps replaced, however there was a lot of touch up work to be done.

LATER THAT MORNING Tesha was outside in her garden. The dirt was soft as she dug a hole to plant the white climbing roses she'd bought from Mrs. Miller. If she were lucky, the weather would not get too hot in the next couple weeks and the plants would have a chance to settle before the heat of summer hit.

Hers would be a calming garden, mostly white flowers to give the space a calming atmosphere. Once both rose plants were in the ground on both sides of her newly built arbor, she began the delicate task of tying the young vines to the bottom of the trellis training them to grow up the structure.

She sat back and admired her work after several minutes. Although most of her plants were still very young, it was easy to tell once they grew in, it would be a wonderful result. A smile tugged at her lips until she glanced through the fencing toward Adam's house.

That afternoon Mrs. Miller and her friends planned to come over. She knew the request of a tour of the house was an excuse. She'd put off meeting the group, not sure if she was ready to make friends and share her life. It was a big step for her; she'd always been the type to keep her circle of friends small.

But today she was glad for the distraction from constantly wondering what Adam was going through. Mrs. Miller and two friends planned to come over and she'd told her they'd bring tea and she'd provide dessert. Not in the mood to bake, she decided to try the new cupcake bakery in town.

SWEET INDULGENCE WAS nestled between a boutique and a gift shop. The store had a welcoming green and grey awning to match the lettering on the cupcake shop's door, which was done in large curly letters.

As soon as she opened the door, Tesha was assaulted by a myriad of amazing aromas. Sweet and appetizing scents mixed to make a wonderful bouquet. Tesha loved the interior immediately. The counters were done in pale blue and yellow and the background wall a dark chocolate with soft polka dots of pink, yellow, blue, and green. There were three ice cream shop style table and chairs sets as well as a large glass display showcasing a wide array of cupcakes.

The intricate design of the toppings was breathtaking. The

young girl behind the counter smiled at her. "I'll be right with you." She was busy with another customer, which gave Tesha more time to study the flavors and décor of the tiny cakes.

"Can I help you?" The girl moved closer to where Tesha stood still undecided at what to choose. She was taller than Tesha, with dark auburn hair that was pulled into a long ponytail. Her green eyes sparkled as she looked down to the cupcakes Tesha had been studying. "Those are my strawberry banana marble." She lifted one from a plate and held it up for Tesha. "I use two kinds of batter. One has banana pulp and the other strawberry flavored cream."

"It sounds delicious. Who owns this place?"

She held up her right hand. "I do."

Tesha couldn't keep the surprise from her voice and expression. "You look so young."

"Cassie Tucker." She held out her hand. "I'm almost thirty. I may look younger thanks to the fact that I rarely have time to put on any make up and spend so much time in here that the sun hasn't touched my skin in months." She laughed. "And any wrinkles probably melt from the heat of the ovens." She grinned and shrugged. "Thanks for the compliment…"

"Tesha." Tesha liked Cassie already. "I'll take a couple of those strawberry cupcakes and what is this?"

They continued on for a bit until Tesha was finally able to choose a dozen cupcakes. She watched Cassie pack them. "I haven't met too many women yet, so Mrs. Miller is bringing her friends over to my place on Magnolia Street tonight for some fun. Would you like to come?"

Cassie's face lit up. "Oh, that's right, you're the one who's redoing the old Victorian on Magnolia aren't you?"

Tesha held her hands up. "Guilty as charged."

"I'm also new to this town. I moved here about a year ago to care for my grandmother after grandpa died."

"That's commendable."

"Not really. It all happened at a time when I needed to leave Nashville and try something new. Bad relationship," Cassie explained.

Tesha decided it was best not to share her own tale of woe. "Please come tonight. They will be there at seven." She paid and lifted the box and then placed it back down. "Can I have one of the red velvet cupcakes for the road?"

Chapter Thirteen

E XASPERATION WAS HEAVY in the air. Both Adam and the psychologist knew it was a colossal waste of time. Each session was the same. A rehashing of every detail that kicked off the not so wonderful movie that his mind insisted on replaying and before the credits finished rolling, the previews began again.

They were in his parents' house, in the den. The familiarity of the space should have put him at ease, but it didn't.

It would be a good idea to tell the older man he wasted his time. Actually the doctor seemed to be a good guy and should call it off himself.

He had to give it to Doctor Mitchell. He maintained a cool reserve, not been at all condescending, and never seemed to lose his patience, even when Adam refused to talk. Or should he say repeat the same shit again. Tired of sitting, Adam slid down a bit and stretched his long legs before him.

Yes, it was juvenile, the posture telling of his boredom, but he couldn't help it. For three weeks, he'd been meeting with this man daily. Every day had turned into something akin to Groundhog Day. Very few variables.

Damn his brothers for bringing him to their parents' house. In the state he'd been in that night, he'd not realized until morning where he was. A flash of brilliance on his brothers' part, but at the same time not a great idea since it hurt their mother to see him that way.

She'd burst out sobbing so hard he'd been shocked into reality. In that instant he'd heard her crying, Adam pulled himself back and tried to console her. But she'd recoiled from him, not sure if he meant to hurt her, his brothers had attacked in force throwing him to the ground and pinning him down until the doctor shot him up with sleepy time crap.

Had to give it to them. They knew what would work. Adam would never rebuff his mother. The next morning he'd woken, Mariam Ford sat at his bedside holding his hand. Her beautiful pale blue eyes welling with tears as she apologized for her reaction the night before. Before she could finish the request, in that instant, he promised to stay as long as it took and agreed to any treatment they decided to try.

"Adam?" Doctor Mitchell frowned. "What are you thinking about?"

"My mother. How heartbroken she'll be when this doesn't work."

"It's too soon to give up, don't you think?" His words grated up and down his skin like sandpaper.

"So this treatment will last longer?" Adam looked past the doctor to the picture on the wall of him and his brothers. It was taken one summer when Tristan had turned eighteen and was ready to leave for college. They'd taken one last family vacation to the gulf coast.

"How are the flashbacks?"

"Same."

Doctor Mitchell made a note. "How many a week?"

"I have to keep them at bay daily."

"Hmm." He wrote another scribble. "Any full blown ones?"

"Not since the other night."

They were silent for a few minutes. The doctor seemed at a loss and Adam agreed with him. It was probably best to stop the waste of time and money.

Doctor Mitchell looked at Adam for a moment. "It occurs to me that we've discussed the rescue. When the medics and injured were struck by sniper fire. You saved four men and flew them to safety." The doctor teetered a pen between two fingers. "Then it stops there, you don't tell me what happened next."

He'd flown half an hour before realizing he was shot. Too scared to look behind him to see if Vince was breathing, he refused to give in to any injury. Vince had been shot up pretty bad. A bloody mess, his face had been unrecognizable when Adam grabbed him and dragged him to the chopper. "I flew them to the medical unit in Kandahar."

"Did you stay?" Doctor Mitchell remained in a relaxed position, but he stopped flipping the pen and was poised to write.

"Yes." Adam laid his head on the back of the chair and looked up at the ceiling. "Look, Doc. It's been almost an hour…"

"How long?"

"What?"

The doctor checked his watch and made a quick note, not seeming to be paying Adam much attention. He looked over at him. "How long did you stay at the medical unit? Why were you there?"

"Two weeks, maybe three. Shot twice in my thigh."

"Hmm." The pen flew across the room. Adam frowned and waited for whatever the doctor planned to do next. Had the man lost it? Adam pushed up and sat upright in the chair. The doctor stood and went to retrieve the pen. "I think we're on to something here."

"Throwing pens?" Adam kept an eye on the doctor's progress in case he decided to throw it his way. "I don't see what that does to help, but you're the doc."

"Sorry, I threw the pen because I'm irate with myself not to have explored this sooner." The doctor sat on the edge of his seat. "Tell me about the hospital."

Adam exhaled. "I had to go under so they could get the bullets and fragments removed from my upper thigh. There was some damage to my side, but it was mostly flesh wounds."

Several questions later, Adam had relaxed into the chair. The doctor was back to flipping the pen and finally it seemed their session was coming to an end. Doctor Mitchell looked at his watch. "What about your friends? Did they all survive?"

"Only one of them was my friend. The other three I didn't know."

"Did he live?" Doctor Mitchell no longer held the pen, but had laid it on top of his notebook.

"No. He did not." Adam's chest constricted, he had to open his mouth to catch a full breath.

The doctor persisted. "Did you speak to him before he died?"

"Yes." More tightening. He had to get out of there.

"What did you talk about?"

"Doc, I have to go." He would have stood, but his legs

trembled from the effort of maintaining his breathing under control. The air became scarce and beads of sweat tricked from his forehead down his temples. "Nothing happened."

"But you did speak to him. What did he say?"

Vince had been so pale, his skin almost translucent. The usual easy grin was gone, the light in his eyes replaced by dullness. There were so many wires, tubes and machines.

The noise had annoyed Adam to no end. Especially when Vince tried to talk. It was hard to hear. "He thanked me."

"For saving his life."

"I didn't save his life."

"You gave him a few precious days. Perhaps time to talk to loved ones."

"His dad, yeah."

"So, that was something."

Adam squeezed his eyes shut. The pounding in his ears would not be quieted. If he were alone, he would sit in the corner and cover his head and hum or something. "I suppose."

"Your friend…"

"Vince."

"Your friend, Vince, did he ask you anything?"

Adam didn't want to remember the conversation. He'd relived it too many times in his mind already. His heart began to hammer against his breastbone and his breathing became shallow. The doctor neared and spoke slowly. "Take a deep breath, Adam." He attempted twice before he was able to breathe almost normally. "Now look at me and focus on this." The doctor held the pen between his fingers and swung it slowly like a pendulum.

"Tell me now, what did Vince ask you?"

"To finish what he couldn't. Renovate the house. Restore the car. The trifecta."

The doctor sat back down. "So your friend had a life plan."

"That's all he talked about."

"Did you do it?"

"Two of the things, I did. I finished the house and restored the damn car. I love that damn car." Adam actually chuckled. "It's a '65 Ford Fairlane."

"Nice." Doctor Mitchell nodded and smiled. "What about the third item on the list?"

"He planned to find a hot girl and marry her. She'd fall in love with him after seeing the car and the house."

Doctor Mitchell frowned. "Seems a lot to ask don't you think?"

What the fuck did this guy know anyway? Adam wanted to punch him. "No, I don't think so. He died. I couldn't save him. He died. I failed him. So it wasn't too much to ask."

"What about your life? What did you want to do when you returned from the war?"

"I have my life."

"Who killed Vince?"

"I think our time's up, doc."

Doctor Mitchell crossed his legs. "I don't have any plans, so no hurry. I would like a cup of coffee in a bit though." He cocked his head and studied Adam. "Who killed Vince?"

"The fucker hiding in the fucking rocks."

"That's correct. So how did you fail Vince?"

"I promised him to finish the trifecta. It was his last request."

"Let's say you found a woman and married her. Moved her

into the house and drove her around in that fancy car. What then?"

"It's not going to happen. I can barely function, much less bring someone else into the house. I won't subject a woman to my night terrors and flashbacks." He hated that an image of Tesha came to the forefront of his thoughts. He hated to not know how she was. He missed her.

"Even without PTSD, you can't live Vince's life for him. He wouldn't have wanted you to."

"You weren't there. He said 'You have to make the most out of your life. Live not just your life to the fullest, but mine for me, too."

"Was your friend a selfish man?"

"No. Of course not."

"Do you really think he intended for you to sacrifice your dreams and plans for him? Do you seriously believe Vince wanted you to move into his house, drive his car and marry the woman he may have married?"

His body deflated. Almost as if someone let all the air out of balloon, Adam melted back into the chair.

"Answer me, Adam. Is that what Vince wanted?" The doctor jotted a quick note. "You see, I think he was encouraging you to have a good life. But did not intend for you to give up your life for what he planned."

"He left me the house and the car."

"Because he cared for you. He gave you what he treasured the most."

It made sense. He and Vince were very close and relied on each other for everything. He'd never make another friend like Vince, no matter how long he lived. Tears welled in his eyes and he didn't try to hide them. "I miss him. It was his day off. He came along for the ride to help out and…"

"He did it because he was your friend."

"We planned to hang out afterwards." Tears trailed down his face. "It's not fair."

"What did you plan to do after the war?"

Adam wiped the back of his hand across his face and let out a breath. "Go back to Nashville. Help my brother at Ford Industries. Buy a new Jag. Date a hot girl."

"So there you have it. Your own trifecta."

"I suppose so. Damn. I hadn't thought about that." Adam sniffed and tried to hide it by clearing his throat. "What about Vince's house?"

"That part he left up to you." The doctor let out a breath. "I didn't know Vince, but it seems to me, he wanted to give you options. Did not mean for you to finish his plans."

The doctor gazed past him and it was then that Adam saw the look he recognized.

"Who did you lose?"

"My son was killed in a roadside bombing in Iraq." The doctor gave him a sad smile.

"I would have given anything to have had the chance to say goodbye. Do you understand what a gift you gave Vince and his father?"

It took a minute for it to sink in and Adam nodded. "Yes, sir, I understand."

Chapter Fourteen

TESHA OPENED THE front door to four women. Mrs. Miller and two friends along with Cassie who held a box of cupcakes. "Surprise! Happy birthday!" they yelled in unison.

They each hugged her as they traipsed in. Cassie pushed Tesha into a chair. "You relax. We brought the party."

Wine was poured. Mrs. Miller arranged the cupcakes on a tray while the other two ladies piled Chinese food onto plates that were passed around. Before long, the women were laughing and prodding Cassie to share her now famous bad date stories. Tesha looked around the table at Mrs. Miller, her friends Carol and Debbie and lastly to Cassie who waddled around imitating some guy's walk, and her heart expanded.

Women knew what it was like to be alone on a birthday, no one to share the special day with. It turned out Carol and Debbie were also widows. So they'd formed a bond of sorts.

"What about you, Tesha?" Mrs. Miller prodded. "I'm sure you had a date gone wrong."

"I did." Tesha took a swallow of wine. "The first time I went out with a guy after David died. He ordered steak the same as David and I began bawling. I couldn't stop crying. You should have seen the look on the poor guy's face. And then his expression tickled me so much I started laughing hysterically. To top it off, I drank my wine in two gulps and ordered three more glasses. By the end of the night my eyes were swollen, my makeup gone and I was drunk." She waited for the women to stop laughing. "I can't imagine why he didn't call me again?"

Mrs. Miller burped and they erupted into fits of giggles. "At least you girls haven't tried dating in your sixties. Carol and I went on a double date, both our dates fell asleep during the movie. When the movie ended my date wouldn't wake up so after ensuring he was still alive. I left him there." Once again they burst into laughter.

Cassie handed Tesha a small bag. "Happy birthday."

Tesha dug out a small stained glass teapot that twirled on a wire. "It's beautiful. Thank you." The overhead light caught the glass perfectly sending reflections around the room.

The women watched in anticipation as she opened the next present, a rectangular cardboard box tied with a blue mesh ribbon. Nestled in the box was a carved hand painted wooden sign with the words *The Haven* etched into the wood.

Tesha sniffed as she held it up. "It's beautiful, I love it. I knew the house would name itself."

"I remember you saying you weren't sure what you planned to call this house." Mrs. Miller smiled brightly. "We thought this was an appropriate name, since Eve was the first woman. I bet she needed a place to get away from Adam. Carol, Debbie, and I ordered it a week ago from a local artist. He did a great job."

"I absolutely love the name." Tesha meant it. "I'm going to get Mr. Shanty to put it up by the front door."

"There's more," Mrs. Miller looked to Debbie. "Tell her."

Debbie a retired schoolteacher smiled widely. "The girls

and I plan to volunteer here the week the widows arrive. We will be here to help for a couple hours each day, provide a shoulder to cry on, someone to talk to, that sort of thing."

"Oh…" Tesha didn't hold back the tears this time. "That's the best present ever." She grabbed the tissue Cassie proffered.

Mrs. Miller's eyes were shiny with unshed tears. "It gives us something to do besides harass Gus at the Bingo Palace."

Cassie stayed behind after the older ladies left. She and Tesha sat on the couch and watched entertainment television. Cassie sipped from her drink. "I may have to stay here. It's only five miles to town, but Deputy Castro is always parked on the side of the road right before getting into town."

"Isn't he the one asked you out?" Tesha laughed. "He's kinda cute."

"He's annoying," Cassie replied and attempted a stern expression, but failed. "Okay, he's sort of cute."

"I'd feel better if you stayed." Tesha assured Cassie when her friend yawned.

IT WAS LATE afternoon as Tesha worked in the garden. It was a quiet day since Mr. Shanty had finished the last tasks she'd given him. She planned a trip to Nashville to purchase furniture the following week to furnish the upstairs rooms. Since she wanted to fill them with vintage like items, she figured the bigger cities would have better options. The sounds of the leaves rustling made her jump back. The last thing she needed was to get bitten by some sort of venomous snake while alone.

A mixed breed brown puppy burst through the plants and headed straight for Tesha. She laughed when it hopped up and down in joyous puppy dance at finding her. "Well, hello there. Who do you belong to?"

"Adam Ford." A man entered the garden with a leash in his hand. He gave her a boyish grin. "Sorry, I thought it would be okay to let her off the leash."

Tesha picked up the puppy that was delighted to finally reach her cheek to lick. "She's so cute. I don't think Adam has a dog."

"I'm James Malloy, here to deliver Ford's dog. My parents saved this little girl for him." His light brown eyes crinkled in the corners when he smiled. "She'll be a surprise I'm sure since he expected a Shepard, but they stopped breeding dogs and gave the last one away since I last talked to Ford. Found this girl at the shelter I volunteer at. She's always happy."

Tesha placed the puppy down and it scampered to explore the garden. "I'm Tesha. I would shake your hand, but as you can see, they're very dirty."

"Ford was supposed to come and pick her up. Since he didn't come to get her and I have to leave for an extended business trip, I brought her here instead only to find him gone." He looked towards Adam's house. "Any idea where he is?"

"He's in Nashville. A family situation I believe."

James had a pained expression when he looked to the puppy. "I don't know what to do. I might have to drop her back off at a shelter."

"No!" Tesha frowned up at him. "How could you do that?"

"I'm a private pilot. I have a six-week assignment on the west coast. I'm flying out in the morning."

"I'll take her." Tesha was not about to allow the beautiful

puppy to spend one night in a horrible shelter. "When Adam returns, he can claim her. If he doesn't then I'll keep her." She gave James a triumphant smile. "I may just keep her anyway. I think he was expecting the larger dog."

James's eyes locked with hers and he nodded. "Sounds good to me." His eyes flickered to her left hand. "Can I take you to dinner to celebrate your new dog?"

Her stomach flipped. The last thing she expected was a date. Not to mention a handsome pilot who actually came to her. A friend of Adam's, so probably a horrible idea. She opened her mouth to tell him no, but instead, "Sure. Sounds great," came out.

"Can I pick you up at seven?"

Once James left, Tesha went inside to find the keys to Adam's house. If he planned to get a dog, he must have acquired the essentials. At least that's what she hoped, not wanting to trudge into town when she had a date to get ready for.

She walked across the lawn towards Adam's house, the puppy bouncing beside her. When she opened the front door, the emptiness of the house made her waiver. "I'll just get your things and we'll leave, okay, girl?" Tesha spoke to the little dog that had no qualms about entering and rushed in and promptly began to sniff the floor.

Thankfully Adam had bought a crate, a bed, dishes and a large bag of puppy food. Tesha made two trips back to her house carrying the items. She refused to stop and look around. It was not the time to acknowledge how much the space reminded her of him. The smell of the house, the shirt thrown over the back of a chair all made her want to stop and sit for a bit. To explore the bedroom to check how much damage they'd caused. Not today, it would be a mistake.

In almost three weeks, Adam had not called or attempted to contact her through his brothers. From the one phone call from Caden, she learned he was at his parents' home outside Nashville and doing well. Other than asking her the status of the house, Caden had not said anything else about his brother.

If she were honest, Adam didn't owe her anything. They'd never clarified their relationship. No strings attached she supposed. Besides what would he say? "I'm in therapy because of you?"

She closed and locked the door behind her and headed back with the puppy at her heels. The bundle of energy rushed back and forth in front of her, one ear flopped down, the other sticking up, and Tesha had to admit it helped brighten her spirits. "I think I want to keep you regardless."

She carried the dog bed and placed the puppy on it. "I have to get ready for a date. How about you hang out with me until I leave?"

The woman in the mirror did not look thrilled at the prospect. "Get over it." Tesha told the reflection. "Maybe it's time to move on."

TWO DAYS LATER, Tesha walked around the open space between the kitchen and the living room and adjusted the pillows on the couches one last time. On the wall behind the couch, a large painting of a woman reading in a garden got her attention next. She moved to it and touched the corner ensuring it was straight. She took a fortifying breath when the sleek Cadillac SUV pulled into the driveway and under her newly constructed carport. From where she stood she could see through the large windows in her office. In the vehicle her parents talked. Well, her mother did most of the talking with her father nodding.

Of course, they had to have a game plan for talking her out of living in Lovely. Her mother's excuse of some fabulous news was no doubt a tactic to bring her back to Georgia. She'd lost track of most of her friends in Atlanta since David's passing. The only one she kept in touch with since moving to Tennessee was Cleve who she spoke with on the phone weekly. There was very little to return to in Atlanta.

She looked around the expanse of her new home. Beautiful moldings framed the ceilings circling each room painted in pristine white to show off the tan color of the space. The combination of old and new came together perfectly.

She inhaled letting the air out slowly as she made her way to the door and opened it as her parents came up the stairs. The puppy that she named Kylie, ran to the door and began to bark while hopping up and down.

Her mother burst in first. "Oh my goodness, Tesha, you look amazing. I missed you so much." Her Hispanic accent fell over Tesha instantly relaxing her. Her mother's familiar Dior perfume surrounded her as she was pulled into a firm hug.

"Should I go back to the car?" Her father joked when her mother continued to hug her. His hazel eyes were warm when meeting Tesha's. He shook his head when her mother finally released her but held onto her hand. "I haven't seen my baby in months, now don't hurry me, Robert."

Tesha threw herself into her father's arms, trying hard not to cry when he patted her back awkwardly as he always did. She kissed his cheek and he chuckled. "Looks like our girl missed us too."

Kylie barked and her father bent to pick her up. "Well, hello there, pup."

"It's beautiful, Tesh." Her mother was already walking about, peeking in doorways and taking in all the décor. "You do amazing work. When you sell, you will be able to demand a great price." Her heels clacked on the wooden floors as she disappeared down the hall. "Oh Robert, come look at this amazing laundry room," she called from the room behind the kitchen.

"We may as well join her," her father said and they walked in the direction of the room.

When the tour of the home was over, Tesha beamed with pride at her mother's compliments and admiration of her work. Her mother didn't miss a single detail, commenting on Tesha's decisions in each room. Finally sipping sweet tea, they sat at the table overlooking the garden where the puppy ran in circles chasing a butterfly.

Her mother pointed out the door. "I'm going there next." Her parents were relatively young, as they'd had Tesha when her mother, Lorena, was only eighteen and her father twenty. They'd met when his family had gone on vacation to the Cabo St Lucas in Baja Peninsula. It was a summer love fling.

After finding out the girl he'd left behind was pregnant, her father managed to find a way to return to Mexico and marry her. Tesha always found their story romantic.

"What is this fabulous news you two have?" Tesha took in her mother whose flawless tanned skin stood out against the turquoise fabric of her vintage Gucci shift dress.

Her mother's bracelets tingled against each other as she

placed her hand over her chest and leaned forward to look at her father. "Should I tell her or you?"

Her father chuckled. "I think it's best you do."

"Tell me already," Tesha huffed. "What are you two up to?"

"We're going to be on television!" Her mother exclaimed while clapping her hands. "On one of my favorite programs, House Buyers International. You know I watch that show all the time."

Tesha couldn't help but laugh at her mother's excitement. "Seriously?"

"Yes, and don't laugh. It's a very popular show." Her mother giggled, her eyes shining brightly. "I'm so excited."

The fact that her mother was excited was easy to understand, but Tesha's father had always been on the quiet shy side. She looked to him. "I can't believe you agreed to this. You're going to have to interact and be talkative on the show, Dad."

The sun shined through the French doors highlighting the soft sprinkling of grey in her father's otherwise black curly hair. He wore a mustache and kept a five o'clock shadow on his face, and with dark chestnut skin, it gave him a handsome without trying look. There was no mistaking the love when he looked at her mom. "Your mother's thrilled. I'll just grunt and nod."

"Wait." Tesha held her hands up. "Did you say international? You're moving away?"

"Only for part of the year," her mother explained and clasped her hands in front of her chest while smiling broadly. "We're buying a vacation home near Lake Chapala," she explained. Lake Chapala was in the interior of Mexico, near

Guadalajara where most of her mother's relatives lived. Her parents and she had gone there often.

Tesha let out a squeal and jumped from her seat to hug her mother who also got up. They held hands and turned in a circle. "I'm so excited. A place to call home in Mexico is amazing. Oh. My. God."

After a dinner of baked chicken and salad Tesha prepared for her parents, they relaxed in the living room. Her father watched the sports channel with Kylie in his lap, while Tesha and her mother looked at the laptop screen at pictures of houses in Mexico. Her mother placed a hand over hers. "You can come and stay in Atlanta in the house while we're gone, if you're ready to come home."

Although she knew the subject would come up, she couldn't help the defensiveness that rose. "This is my home now, Mami."

"I know you feel that way, honey, but your career won't flourish here. The market changes and you have to stay abreast of what's current. You certainly can't do it here in this small town." Her mother's real estate side came out as she surveyed the surroundings.

"I am not sure I want to do modern design anymore. I may have found my calling in vintage, old houses and such."

"There are plenty of older homes to decorate in Atlanta and the surrounding areas. I worry about you being alone here in this remote area. What about friends? Do you date? You're much too young to be a hermit."

Tesha laughed. "Mom, I'm not a recluse. Although I do admit I have spent more time home than ever, but I've met some nice ladies and I've even gone on a date. With a pilot."

"Oh, do tell." Her mother pursed her lips and lifted an eyebrow in disbelief. "Did he fly into the empty field across the street?"

Both giggled.

"No, Mami, we went out to dinner."

Tesha told her about James and how he came to bring the puppy to her neighbor who was gone. She was purposely evasive about Adam, not wanting to give her mother any inkling about what transpired between her and the hunky neighbor. She explained how Adam expected a German Shepard, so she was pretty sure he'd not have a problem with her keeping Kylie. After that, she told her mother about Cassie and Mrs. Miller and how they'd come to celebrate her birthday.

Although appeased, it was obvious her mother continued to think she was wasting away in Lovely. She tapped her finger on the coffee table. "I understand what you're trying to do here, I really do. But by bringing hurting widows, I'm afraid it will cause you to relive your grief, sending you backwards instead of moving forward."

Tesha considered the truth in her mother's words. How would looking into the raw pain of a recent loss affect her? She hadn't considered it. "I'll think about it and maybe restructure my plans. I have several women who have volunteered to help. It will only be for one week a year, so I don't have to be here." Her mind reeled with new possibilities, but at the same time, she decided that while others would pay, widows would come free of charge.

"Robert, I almost forgot the gift we brought." Her mother knew exactly when to pull back and let her Tesha off the hook.

Her parents went outside while Tesha obediently sat on the couch not looking out the windows. Her mother came and took her hand. "Come outside."

In the corner of the garden her parents had placed a tall-carved wooden angel that held its hands open, wings stretched out. It fit perfectly amongst the flowering bushes. Her mouth fell open at a beautiful chair made of branches placed next to it. The wide armrests perfect to hold a book or cup.

She turned to her mother a tear escaping the corner of her eye. "It's perfect."

"We do support you, honey. I understand what you're doing here. But I also miss you terribly." They hugged while her father and the puppy walked out of the garden toward the back of the house. Tesha suspected he planned to take advantage and smoke without her mother's reproach.

"The white hydrangeas are beautiful," her mother told her as she settled into one of the wicker chairs outside the French doors. "I didn't know you gardened."

Tesha sipped her iced tea. "I started container gardening in Atlanta, Mami. I was surprised by how much I enjoyed it and decided to go bigger here. I find it relaxing. Honestly I didn't expect the plants to flourish like they have. And I have to admit, I've had a lot of help from Mrs. Miller."

The breeze stirred and the wind chimes she'd recently installed tinkled. Her mother looked across the way to where the puppy now slept. "I can see how you love it here. But this is a life for an older woman, Tesh. Consider it a vacation. You are young, vibrant, and full of life. Have always enjoyed an active life, nightclubs, nice restaurants and sporty cars. I don't see you staying her forever."

"Neither do I, honestly." Something in her chest constricted when catching sight of Adam's house. "But for now, it's what I need. Don't worry about me, Mom. I promise I'm still me. My plan is to stay here for two or three years. At that time, I'll decide whether to live here or get the B&B going, find someone to take it over and keep it as a business or maybe sell it. I will decide when the time is right."

"Regardless of anything, I expect you in Atlanta in August. We always attend the wine festival together. Since we missed it last year, we have much to make up for."

"Of course, nothing can drag me away from endless wine." Tesha missed spending quiet time with her mother. They were close as she was their only child. It made living away from Atlanta harder, but at the same time, it helped her move past the melancholy that had stuck to her like a thick coat of paint. "I miss you, Mami."

"We'll spend time together in August and once we buy the house in Lake Chapala, promise me you'll come and stay for a bit."

"Of course."

"Now, tell me about your pilot."

Oh, boy. Her date with James Malloy had been nice, but nothing spectacular. He'd called a couple times to ask about Kylie, but they'd not made plans for another date, especially since he was in the west coast for another four months.

"He's a very nice man. Tall…"

Chapter Fifteen

ADAM WALKED INTO the music room surprised to find it empty. Caden was usually strumming on a guitar or on the drums in the evenings.

"Hey, son," Roman Ford walked in behind him and went directly to his guitar. "Planning to play?"

He'd not picked up a guitar in years and didn't plan to start now. He wasn't sure why he'd even walked in there. Probably for different scenery, since he'd been stuck indoors for the last couple days as summer storms raged outside. A familiar tune filled the room and he sat to listen. "Remember when we planned to start a band?"

"Yep," his father replied with a smile. "You boys were pretty serious there for a while. Practiced every day."

"We thought we'd be rock stars. Planned on it. We may have done it if Jensen didn't insist on being the lead singer."

Roman Ford laughed. "He's a clown. Tristan has a much better singing voice. But that boy was too shy to perform."

"Did I hear my name?" Tristan stood at the door. Still in his business suit, he held a briefcase in one hand and raked the other one through his wet hair. "It's a doozy out there."

"You gonna play?" Tristan looked to Adam. "Haven't heard you play in a long time."

"That's because I haven't. Probably take me some time to

get back into it."

"You're a great guitarist." Tristan placed the briefcase on the floor and walked in pulling the suit jacket off. He grabbed Adam's old guitar and strummed it. It was tuned.

"Who's been playing my guitar?" Adam instantly got up and snatched it from Tristan. "You've got your own."

"Not me," Tristan replied already picking up his own base guitar. "Probably Caden."

"Caden!" Adam hollered.

The youngest Ford looked over. "What?"

"Why are you always here?" Tristan asked, not giving Adam a chance to get onto him about borrowing his guitar. "Every time I stop by you're here."

Caden shrugged.

"He's living here," their father said still strumming the guitar. "His girlfriend kicked him out. Said he was spoiled rotten."

Caden rolled his eyes and leaned on the doorjamb. "I don't know why she had to go and call Mom."

"She called Mom?" Tristan began to laugh. "Boy, she really was mad at you."

"Yeah." Caden sat behind the drums. "I still have some stuff over there. But she changed the locks, so I can't get in."

Everyone except for Caden laughed. He scowled. "It's not funny, my Bose headphones are over there."

"Why don't you get your own place?" Adam had to ask. "You're a detective now, I'm sure you can afford it. Not to mention all the money Jensen and Tristan always throw at you."

"He's too lazy," their mother said from the door. "I keep

telling your father we need to give him an ultimatum and kick him out to find a place."

Everyone looked at Caden, who remained frozen, his eyes wide. He recovered and managed an indignant expression. "I'll get a place as soon as I finish this assignment. And y'all will have to cough up some awesome housewarming presents from the list I'll give you."

"You need to settle down." Their mother's gaze swept over her sons. "All of you do. Tristan, you're almost forty and still single."

"I'm thirty-eight."

"Like I said, almost forty. Caden, you need a woman who will set your straight. You're a spoiled brat thanks to your brothers and us." She gave her husband a pointed look and then cocked her head to the side and studied Adam last. "Now you. Something's there, you have a settled and in love look about you."

His brothers stared at him and Adam looked around the room. "I don't look settled and in love."

"Well, you must have someone in mind," his mother insisted. She shrugged. "Fine, don't tell me. Boys come on, time to make the salad. I'm having a drink of wine while you get dinner on the table."

It was a family tradition. They had specific chores after their mother cooked the main meal. It gave her time to relax a few minutes before dinner.

Adam watched his parents walk out together and frowned. What had his mother seen? How would she suspect he was in love?

Tristan nudged him on the shoulder. "I'm glad it's you and

not me."

"Yeah, you got that look," Caden added wiggling his eyebrows. "You look settled."

"Shut up."

After dinner, Adam went to his bedroom. He stared at his cell phone and considered calling Tesha. It had been too long since hearing her voice. The fact that he thought about her daily didn't mean she would know it. The thought of what she'd seen that night made him hesitate every time. He'd attacked her in a jealous rage, had tried to take her against her will. Then how he'd reacted when she attempted to calm him made him put the phone down.

He'd told her to move on, to forget him. Had she? According to Caden, she had only called once to ask about him.

Doctor Mitchell had finally decided he could be left unsupervised. He was free to leave after their next consult. With the promise of meeting with him for therapy twice a week.

Right now, his plan was to return to Ford Industries and get reacquainted with the schedule of working in his old job. According to Dr. Mitchell, he needed daily structure and should plan to return to live in Nashville, to his old life. His current homework assignment was to draw up a plan for that.

What did he want? His career back? He considered moving back into an apartment in the city, not too far from the offices. A house would be better, maybe one with land around it. Although he enjoyed remodeling the Victorian, he preferred a more modern home.

Adam read his notes on the pad of paper on the nightstand. The short list, had most items crossed out. How had he become so submerged in Vince's life that he'd forgotten his own aspirations?

The paper scratched against the surface of the wood as he slid the pad closer. He wrote Executive at Ford Industries across the top, then listed his plans for a career that included expanding the company further south. His cousin Bradley Ford in Charlotte had expressed an interest in heading that operation.

The pen remained suspended in midair as he searched his mind for more personal items. He wanted a wife and children, but first he had to ensure his PTSD was under control. He now believed it was possible.

Since discussing Vince's last words, he'd not had an attack or flashback. Of course he'd been in a controlled environment. Once he left the walls of his family home, he wasn't so sure they wouldn't return with a vengeance.

He put the pad and pen aside. Damn how he hated not being the firm, strong, self-assured man he once was.

Chapter Sixteen

GROGGY FROM SLEEP and Kylie's insistent barking, Tesha trudged to the side door to let the dog out. She couldn't help but look across the way towards Adam's house. Her heart skipped at beat at seeing his truck parked beside it. He'd come home.

There were no other signs of anything different, the curtains were drawn and from what she could see, he was not outside.

Tesha stumbled backward in her hurry to get back inside. As soon as the dog finished she urgently called to it. "Come on, Kylie, let's go back in."

Of course the puppy paid her no mind, too busy investigating a new smell in the garden. She closed the door and moved away from the windows.

A few minutes later, the puppy barked. The high-pitched yaps, which either signaled a new lizard in the garden or a visitor, made Tesha uneasy. She was not ready to face Adam, didn't know how she'd react.

He stood in the garden, just inside the gate looking down at the puppy that barked and ran circles around his ankles. When she opened the door, he looked up at her. Butterflies fluttered in her belly and she mentally told them to go to hell. It was hard to tell by his expression if he was angry with her or not.

"Hello, Tesha." He looked good. Had gained some weight in the right places, if possible, his shoulders looked broader and his eyes were sharp, some of the wariness gone. One corner of his lips lifted. "I'm sorry not to have called first. I came to check on the house."

The house. Not to see her. Tesha wasn't sure what to say. Her stomach was still doing too many flips for her to concentrate on what he said. "I think the house is fine. I went over a couple times to check."

"How are you?" He didn't move toward her, which she took as a sign she shouldn't move closer either. It surprised her that he'd stop by at all.

She looked for the puppy to tell him the news then realized the dog had slipped back inside through the open door, probably seeking her food bowl for breakfast. "I am good. Are you back to stay?"

She'd forgotten how handsome he was, her daydreams had not done him justice. The darkness of his hair brought out the blue of his eyes. Of course the curves of his sensuous lips were hard to look away from. He'd not shaved, had a couple days growth, which was sexy on him. He wore a grey t-shirt and jeans. Filled both just right. Tesha did a mental headshake. She was standing outside in her pajama pants and tank top with bare feet. Probably not the picture of loveliness. "I hope you understand why I called your brother that night."

Adam nodded, but did not say anything.

She was not playing the silent game with him today. "I'm glad to see you, I better get inside and get dressed."

"I'm not sure when I'll be back." His gaze lingered on hers

and she took a step back. This was not the time to allow him to think that just because he stopped by she'd throw herself at him. "I still have things to work on."

Tesha swallowed. Why was he really there? Although his eyes took her in with what could pass for want, she was not at ease with him today. It would only make things harder for her when he left again. Adam was not telling her anything, not explaining why he came to see her. "Why are you here, Adam?"

"I needed to see you and thank you for calling my brother. It turned out to be a good thing. I also thought…" He shrugged. "I thought you'd like to know I think about you all the time."

"I wondered how you were doing and if you got some counseling. I'm glad to hear it." She ignored the last comment. The pang of discomfort at how distant they were now threatened to turn into pain. "I have to go." She turned and rushed inside ensuring to shut the doors and lock them. Aware he could see her through the French doors, she walked into her bedroom and closed that door as well.

After getting dressed she wandered back to the main rooms. She peered out the window. Adam's truck was gone. Unsure of her plans, Tesha sat on a barstool and looked around the space. God she was lonely, she missed him, wanted him to tell her he cared for her. He'd not said much, which was typical and there could be some satisfaction in him telling her he thought about her. But she wondered if he'd thought by showing up and saying that she'd immediately have sex with him. Was that why he'd come? Hoping to get a piece of ass and then ride off into the sunset again until deciding he needed to get laid again?

A part of her understood if that was the case. After all, she was the first woman he'd slept with more than once since Afghanistan. At least that's what he'd said and she didn't take him for a liar.

Tesha could understand Adam. She'd had a hard time letting go of Cleve after being with him. He was her first lover after David's passing. Thank God they were able to remain friends and she didn't lose him. But with Adam it was totally different, she could never be just friends with him.

An hour later, she entered Cassie's shop. The sugary smell in the air made her mouth water. Cassie looked up from behind the counter where she was setting up a display of what looked to be birthday cupcakes. "Good morning, Tesha. Good timing, I can use your taste buds."

Tesha chuckled. "Am I that easy?"

"When it comes to cupcakes, yes." Cassie rushed into her kitchen and came back with two cupcakes. They were undecorated with a sort of glaze on top. "It's my new recipe. Ooooey Gooey Caramel. The batter is butter crème, in the center there is melted caramel and over the top a caramel glaze."

They sat at one of her small tables with a cup of coffee and one cupcake each. Both were silent, taking the taste testing very seriously. Tesha allowed the creaminess to linger on her tongue. She closed her eyes and tasted the wonderful mixture of butter and caramel. "These are wonderful. I think I have a new favorite."

"They are good," Cassie mumbled, her mouth still full. She patted herself on the back. "I'm a genius."

"And modest too," Tesha said while licking the last of the

confection off her fingers.

"Something's wrong." Cassie studied her for a moment. "Usually after eating a cupcake, you get a goofy look. You are not looking goofy right now."

Tesha wanted to deny that even the wonderful cupcake had barely lifted her spirits. "Adam came to see me this morning."

"Oh my God, did he take Kylie?" Cassie's eyes were wide.

"No, actually I forgot to tell him about her. He came to tell me he was staying in Nashville a bit longer. Actually, I'm not sure why he came by."

Understanding dawned by the way Cassie's let out a breath and her eyes softened. "It was hard seeing him then?"

"Yes. I wish he'd not stopped by at all."

"Did he say something about where you stand with him?"

"He said he missed me. But I'm not sure how to take that. I ran in the house, had to get away from him before I did something stupid."

Cassie's hand was warm when she patted her upper arm. "I'm sorry. Love stinks."

Love? "Men stink." Tesha looked toward the display. "I need another cupcake."

She chose a red velvet one and broke it in half, then placed the second half in front of Cassie. "Why don't you date anyone?"

"Because of my wedding day." Cassie shook her head. "I didn't dump my last boyfriend. He was my fiancé. So cliché really, catching him with someone, in our apartment, a woman I thought was my friend."

"No!" Tesha exclaimed. "That is horrible."

"Tell me about it. I came home from work early and caught him with his dick hanging out. They were in our bed. Good thing I refrained from grabbing a knife and cutting it off."

"What did you do?"

Cassie chuckled and let out a breath. "It would make a good movie scene. They were so engrossed; they didn't see me come in. I always keep a decanter of water on a nightstand. I threw it all over them. Then I called his mother, who was supposed to come over so we could shop for wedding stuff and told her I'd just caught Kevin and Angela fucking in our bedroom."

"Wow." Tesha sat back. "I can't imagine what you felt."

"Anger mostly. The hurt came later. My parents came to get me and drove me home, I was pitching a fit, cussing, screaming, and crying all at once. I don't remember much about later that night except crying in bed. At least he did have the decency to repay my part for the cost of the wedding."

"Did he try to talk to you after?"

From Cassie's expression, Tesha could tell the memory still hurt. "He did. Called, texted, came to my parent's house, my job. He apologized many times. Never really explained why he did it, other than to say it was the stupidest thing he'd ever done. He tried to convince me to work things out, but when I couldn't get over it."

They continued to sit in companionable silence until a customer came in. Tesha watched Cassie's interaction with the woman who had a hard time deciding between the many choices and ended up buying twice what she'd originally said she needed. Cassie was a great woman, pretty and with a good heart. Whoever Kevin was had lost out on a great thing.

A black Ford F250 drove past. Adam was still in town it seemed. He parked in front of the hardware store. He got out of the truck, seemed to hesitate at the door and then went inside.

"I'm going to hang out here a bit longer," Tesha, told Cassie who'd also watched Adam through the window.

"Good idea."

Chapter Seventeen

THE SUN WAS setting as Adam drove along a two-lane highway. It was not a long drive to Nashville, but for the route he chose, a long-winding road, it would take an additional hour to arrive at his parents' home. It suited him just fine, needed the time to think and clear his head. Besides, he preferred the less traveled roads.

In the back of the truck flowers were secured against the cab. He'd almost forgotten to get the rose bushes his mother specifically asked him to pick up from Miller Hardware on his way home. Thankfully Mrs. Miller had four plants on hand, so at least one person would be happy with him today.

It had been a mistake to see Tesha. He waged an internal war since leaving her garden to go back and make her understand how much he missed her. He should have told her how he truly felt. Kissed her until they were both breathless.

She didn't trust him that much was obvious from the way she kept moving backward. After seeing him at his worst he didn't blame her, no woman would want a broken piece of shit like him.

Even though the flashbacks seemed to have stopped for now. It was hard to be hopeful, if he got better, returned to Nashville, then maybe he'd allow himself the luxury to think of a future. Right now, it felt more like limbo.

He flipped through the radio stations and settled for one, Bruno Mars began to croon and Adam had to agree. There was nothing he would change about Tesha. Well, maybe one thing. For her to give him a second chance.

"Would you like to sit in on the meeting?" Tristan, who sat behind his desk, asked Adam a few days later, as his secretary handed him a folder with papers to sign. "You can listen in, don't have to participate. Start getting in the loop of things."

Adam held copies of the plans for the southeast expansion that he planned to read over. "I'd like to, yes. It's at two this afternoon, right?"

Although his brother's head was bent as he read the paperwork he nodded. "Yes, at two."

Adam walked back to his office that overlooked the Titan's stadium and stood at the window, peering down at the view.

"Adam, you have a phone call," Tristan's secretary poked her head in the doorway.

"It's about time you get back to work, Ford," Malloy's voice brought Adam upright. The familiar sound bringing back his time in Afghanistan. Malloy was one of the injured men he'd rescued that fate-filled day. He'd emailed back and forth with Malloy about the dog, but through all the counseling and starting back at work, he'd totally forgotten about it.

"I totally forgot about the dog," Adam said, feeling guilty. "I had to come to Nashville unexpectedly that weekend."

Malloy's familiar chuckle made him want to smile. "It's good. Don't worry. Tesha is already in love with the pup and says she plans to keep it."

Tesha? "Tesha? How did you—"

Malloy interrupted. "I brought Kylie, as she named it, to drop her off a few weeks back and you weren't home. I met Tesha, she said she'd keep the dog until you return." The pup he'd seen the day he stopped by. It must have been Malloy's gift. "I thought you were giving me a purebred German Shepard."

"I was, but my parents don't breed them anymore." Malloy cleared his throat. "Anyway. That's not what I called about. I'm calling about some business. I'm going to be in town. I grabbed an opportunity to fly back to Tennessee. Needed an excuse to see Tesha again."

Adam tried to remain civil. "See Tesha about what?"

"Oh, of course, you may not have seen her since you're in Nashville. We went out to dinner and have been keeping in touch. She's a beauty. I'm very interested."

Fuck. Adam ground his teeth. "What kind of business are you proposing?"

While Malloy talked about the possibility of Ford Industries marketing for a new transporting shipment company, Adam wanted to stop him and demand to know what transpired between him and Tesha. He had no right, but that didn't stop him from being jealous.

Finally after arranging for Malloy to meet with Tristan and him the following week, he hung up.

His cell phone lay on his desk as he contemplated calling Tesha. It would make sense that she moved on. It was a bit over a month since he'd left. She'd kept in touch with Malloy. What did that mean?

Why did he feel so annoyed? He'd told her to move on, had not kept in touch with her. Hell, he was too mixed up inside for it to make any sense. He pushed the phone away just as Tristan knocked. "They're here. The Vandericks. Father and daughter."

He picked up his iPad and walked with Tristan to the conference room. If the Vandericks agreed to their deal on marketing their publishing company, it would be a multi-million dollar deal.

In the conference room they sat around a large table. Tristan and Adam sat on one side, the Vandericks across from them and two other managers.

Alana Vanderick was a striking blonde who had a reputation for being ruthless when it came to business. Halfway through the meeting, he was not impressed by her, but instead found her condescending and snobby. Her father attempted to get her to back down a couple of times without success. Finally, they came to an agreement after three hours of negotiating.

Alana smiled at Adam, reminding him of a piranha. "How about dinner to celebrate? My treat."

He started to say no, but Tristan cleared his throat and gave him a pointed look.

"It would be my pleasure."

DINNER WENT WELL, at least better than Adam expected. Alana loosened up and kept the conversation away from business. She flirted continuously, but it was easy for Adam to keep her at arm's length. As soon as this dinner was over, he planned to drive straight to Lovely and talk to Tesha. Figure things out between them once and for all.

Over dessert, Alana insisted they share, she finally broached the subject why she'd asked him to dinner.

"I want to go to bed with you. You're not dating anyone are you?" A woman used to getting her way, her lips curved up at his surprised expression. "I'm staying close to here tonight, just up the street at Union Station. Top floor."

Adam wondered how to extract himself from the situation without hurting the company. Before he probably wouldn't have turned her down. He gave it all when it came to getting a contract, including his body if it was called for. But in this instance, he couldn't do it. Not only did he have no desire to sleep with anyone other than Tesha, but also he didn't care for Alana in the least.

"I do have someone in my life, currently. I am not free to take you up on your very tempting offer." He took her hand and kissed her knuckles to hopefully keep her from angering.

"Your loss." Alana replied extracting her hand and held it up to get the waiter's attention. "Two martinis please."

It looked like he wouldn't make it to Lovely this night.

Chapter Eighteen

"Now, that's a hunk," Cassie giggled and pointed at the television. "I make it a point to watch every single George Clooney movie."

Tesha walked back from the kitchen with refilled wine glasses. "He's a good looking man, but I prefer Chris Evans."

"Oooh yes, girl." They chatted while watching the entertainment channel and flipping through magazines.

The evening news came on and both looked up with shocked expressions as a merger between Ford Enterprises and Vanderick Incorporated was announced. The newscaster turned to his partner. "To seal the deal, the brother of CEO Tristan Ford, Adam Ford and Alana Vanderick were seen dining at Etch, the swanky downtown restaurant." They flashed a picture of Adam kissing a woman's hand.

Tesha sat forward, her mouth forming an 'O.'

"That was Adam wasn't it?" Cassie blurted and began coughing, choking on her wine.

Tesha's chest hurt when she tried to take a deep breath. "Yes, it was Adam. Seems he's doing well." She fought to swallow, her mouth suddenly parched. "I guess he's moving on, starting over in Nashville."

"I'm sorry, Tesh. I know it hurt to see that."

"Yes, it did."

THE NEXT DAY, Tesha's head felt heavy. She'd drank too much wine after seeing the news report of Adam and the blonde. Seemed blondes were his type. The ex-wife had been a blonde too.

Cassie was gone, she'd left early enough to be at her shop by ten in the morning. It was another hour before Tesha trudged to the kitchen. She took two aspirins with iced tea and slumped into a dining room chair.

The unmistakable rattle of Mr. Shanty's truck came closer until it neared her house. Minutes later Mr. Shanty and Jerry Pike entered, both looked past her with badly concealed interest toward the kitchen. Tesha took pity on them. "I have leftover biscuits from yesterday. How about some coffee while I warm them up and we wait for Mrs. Miller?"

While the men ate, Mr. Shanty explained that Mrs. Miller was meeting them there. They had plans for the upcoming Fourth of July celebration. Neither of the men seemed to know what the plans were, so she gave up asking questions. Finally Mrs. Miller, Carol, and Debbie arrived. They helped themselves to biscuits and before long all were settled around the table.

Mrs. Miller wiped her mouth. "I am going to need all of your help for this Fourth of July town celebration. We're going to have a heroes theme and include a special renaming of the library." Her wide smile made everyone return the gesture although they had no idea what she planned.

An hour later, the people filed out, each with an assignment for the special patriotic celebration. Tesha laughed when Mr. Shanty patted her on the arm. "Thank you for the biscuits. I think you should add that to your list. Provide biscuits for the volunteers."

Tesha laughed. "I'll do it."

They planned to honor Adam by naming the new library after him. Tesha wondered what his reaction would be. Mrs. Miller said she'd asked him to return for the celebration and he'd promised to.

Her cell phone buzzed. It was Jensen Ford.

Chapter Nineteen

"YOU NEED TO get whatever is eating you taken care of and come back when your head is in Ford Enterprises. I need time off and you are not ready to take over yet." Tristan loomed over Adam's desk. It was easy to see how Tristan got things done. Not once had he raised his voice, but Adam got the message loud and clear.

"I can do this, Tristan." Adam glared at his brother.

"No, you can't. Admit it."

"Fine," he relented. "I do have to clear some things up, but I promise you I'll be back and more than ready to do this right." He stood and looked his brother in the eye. "You've been great, Tristan. I'm sorry to have left you with all of this on your shoulders."

His brother nodded. "I had to fire, Dad. He tried to help for the first year, but we argued more than worked."

Adam laughed. "He called me and complained, said we should form a coup against you."

"It's been a long time since I've seen you laugh." Tristan hugged Adam. "Welcome to the land of the living brother."

"Adam, your brother Jenson is on the phone." The secretary's face was flushed. "He sounds so nice."

"He's not," Tristan told her on the way out. "He's a pain in the butt." She shrugged, smiling broadly. "I keep hoping he comes here one day."

Adam picked up the phone to Jenson talking to someone else. "Hello?"

"Hey, bro." Jenson screamed into the phone. "Where are you?"

"At the office." Adam sighed. "Are you drinking?"

"What?" Jenson hollered again. "I can't hear a damn thing. They are hammering and moving furniture in. I had to come open the house. You're not here."

"What the hell are you talking about, Jenson?" Adam stalked to grab his jacket and was already walking to the elevators.

"I can't hear you. I'm at your house. You know, for the movie."

Two hours later, Adam parked across the street from his house. It was the closest he could get. He walked around a moving van and barely missed getting hit with a golf cart with two men hollering into cell phones.

Several people carried chairs and tables into the house while a woman stood on the front porch with a clipboard barking out orders. On the lawn beside the house, a trailer was set up, under its awning several people lazed in lawn chairs drinking cocktails. He stopped short when looking to the other side of his house. There were several bulldozers clearing the vegetation. He ran around the house to go in though the back door. In the backyard another surprise awaited. The dog pen was gone and replaced by what looked to be a miniature restaurant.

A cook waved at him. "Burgers won't be ready until six."

He ignored the man and rushed inside. It took a few minutes to adjust his eyes to the dimmer interior. There were people everywhere. Pictures were being hung, carpets rolled out. Jensen sat on a barstool, on his phone with a beer in front of him. He turned to Adam. "Let me call you back, my brother is finally here." He put the phone down and jumped to his feet.

"Amazing, isn't it?" He held his arms open like a magician finishing a great trick. "You won't recognize it when they're done."

Adam threw a punch first, but Jensen was quick and dodged it. He wasn't fast enough to avoid the tackle though. They tumbled across the floor, while people mostly stepped over them. His brother let out a loud "Oomph" when he punched him in the gut and then got lucky and punched Adam on the side of the face.

The lady with the clipboard came and hit Adam on top of the head with it. "You're in the fucking way. Go play outside."

Both brothers held on to the other's shirt as they stumbled outside.

"What the hell is wrong with you?" Jensen frowned. "You having a flashback or something." He spoke slowly. "Adam, I am your brother Jensen, not Al Qaeda."

"I know who the fuck you are. What are they doing to my house?"

"Making a movie. Remember?" Jensen lunged away from Adam's grasp. "You're crazy." His eyes widened. "Not PTSD crazy. Just crazy, crazy."

Adam shook his head and let out a breath. "They are tearing up the field next to the house, my trees are gone and what the hell is that damn thing doing there?" He pointed to the trailer.

"It's for some of the crew. They will sleep in there." Jensen frowned. "I'm staying in your room, so you'll have to sleep somewhere else."

If he killed his brother, his parents would be angry. Although Jensen was self-absorbed and rarely listened to others, for some reason they loved him. Adam grabbed Jensen by the shoulders. "First of all, I never agreed to this. I realize it's probably too late to tell you and all of them to get the hell off my property. But I swear Jensen when this is done. I'm going to kill you."

In pure Jensen fashion, his brother grinned at him, it was obvious he did not take the threat seriously. "Guess what? They are paying you half a mil, just for this. And you have a walk-on part."

A slight man with tall hair, tight fuchsia pants and horn-rimmed glasses approached. He lifted a hand and held it up as if holding a tray. Adam watched him look between them. "This must be your brother." He stated the obvious while his gaze worked its way down Adam's body. "Yum."

"Adam, this is Stephan Flair, he's the set stylist."

"Of course, he is," Adam mumbled attempting to shake the man's limp hand.

"Jensen a word with you." The golf cart duo approached. Both men held up their cell phones. One was young, perhaps late thirties. His blond hair styled within an inch of its life in a perfect backswept style. The other older man had a receding hairline and orange-tinged skin from obvious artificial tanning. "Jensen," the blonde one called out. "Is that the stunt double you told us about?"

Jensen gave Adam a triumphant look. "Yep, that's my bro. He's a war hero. Adam can fall from tall buildings and land on his feet in a single bound." He looked at Adam and whispered, "You won't have to do that."

The men gave Adam a once over. At the same time the stylist reached up and lifted a chunk of his hair. "I'll have to lighten it."

"Jensen." Adam growled and pushed the style man away and glowered at the men in the golf cart. They scooted off, both with cell phones back on their ears.

"I'd do you, angry man." the stylist blew him a kiss and sashayed away.

"I would say you can stay next door, but my costar and two others are already booked there." Jensen told him while looking around as if deciding where to go.

"At Tesha's?" Adam looked toward the white Victorian. "When did everyone get here?"

"Two days ago," Jensen replied already making his way back inside. "Burgers should be ready in a few. Come on."

Adam walked behind his brother at a loss for what to do. He planned to ensure they did not destroy any of the work he'd done on the house. No matter how much they paid, it would be up to him to repair any damage. He didn't have the time to do more repair work. He'd promised Tristan to work full time at Ford Enterprises.

Jensen was ecstatic over the hamburgers. He grabbed two and began to eat while piling fries on his plate. Adam knew his brother spent the time he didn't work in the gym. It was a good thing since his eating habits were horrible.

"Breakfast is really good here, too," Jensen told him between bites. "Tesha and a woman from town, Cassie I think, took the job."

Great.

Chapter Twenty

TESHA RUSHED PAST Cassie to the ovens. The biscuits were almost done in one and in the other a breakfast casserole was perfectly browned. She hit the 'warm' button. Cassie put carafes of juice on the counter and began placing juice glasses in three perfect rows of five.

She smiled broadly at Tesha. "It's exciting all these famous people here." Cassie began setting up coffee cups with saucers. "I can't believe Adam's brother is Jensen Ford."

"I was shocked the first time I saw him too," Tesha told her and pulled the biscuits from the oven. "He seems nice, too."

"I can't wait to meet him." Cassie pretended to swoon and then gave a soft squeak when the actor and two men entered through the French doors. "Good morning," her friend's voice shook and Tesha fought not to giggle.

"Please help yourselves to juice and coffee. I'll have food on the table in a minute." Tesha was already placing biscuits into a covered basket, while Cassie cut the casserole and placed serving sizes onto small square plates.

Jensen looked past Cassie to Tesha and gave her a signature flirty smile. "Seen my brother?"

Her stomach flipped just from the mention of Adam. "No, is he here?"

"He was here last night. Something's wrong with him, he

was in a mood." Jensen grabbed two biscuits and passed on the casserole. He wagged his eyebrows at Cassie. "Got any dessert?"

Cassie attempted to talk and croaked instead. "There's fruit."

Jensen wrinkled his nose. "Nah, too healthy."

"Cassie owns a cupcake shop in town, we'll bring them over to the dining area later this afternoon."

He seemed appeased. "Awesome."

A flushed Cassie stood frozen until Tesha nudged her. "I think we should refill the juice carafe." Several more people joined the men including two women. One was Jensen's costar, another famous actor, Vanessa Morgan.

While the people ate, Tesha refilled cups and collected plates keeping an eye on the door. If Adam was there, he seemed to be staying away. She went to the French doors and looked outside. She wondered how it would look on the big screen. Right now it looked like a carnival had ascended between the houses.

It turned out perfect for her, giving her three guests for four weeks and a chance to try out her breakfast recipes.

Vanessa Morgan came to stand next to her while sipping on tea. In the two days she'd been there, Tesha had not seen her eat anything more than a bite here and there. She nibbled on fruit or drank some sort of shakes, but other than that sipped on water mostly. She held a teacup up to her lips and followed Tesha's line of vision. "They'll put everything back once we leave, you'll never know we were here."

"I don't think they can replant the trees they are removing." Tesha couldn't help the disappointment in her voice. "I know it's not my property, but I hate to see beautiful healthy trees chopped down."

"Hmm," the actress replied in a noncommittal tone. "I doubt Jensen's crazy brother cares about trees. You should have seen the way he attacked him."

"Adam attacked Jensen?" Tesha's eyes rounded. "Why?"

Vanessa shrugged, "I don't know. They rolled around the floor beating each other until one of our crew broke them up. It was crazy-stupid." She strolled away and began talking to one of the men.

Soon after everyone left to do whatever they did, Tesha remained apprehensive, why had Adam and Jensen fought? Was Adam hurt? She shoved her hands down into the soapy water and huffed. The last thing she needed to do was worry about what Adam did or didn't do. He'd obviously moved on and here she was still mooning over the man.

"I'm going into town to check on things at the shop," Cassie told her as she took her apron off and hung it on a hook inside the pantry door. "I've got the list of groceries to pick up in town, text or call me if you think of something we need." Cassie came to stand closer. "Hey. Are you all right? You're scowling."

"I'm fine." Tesha smiled. "Just figuring out which chore to do next. Ms. Debbie and Carol should be here soon to straighten up the bedrooms, and other than cleaning up here, I pretty much have a free day."

Cassie smiled broadly. "I plan to come back with special cupcakes and go with you next door to deliver them. Maybe catch another glimpse of that yummy Jensen." Her enthusiasm was contagious and Tesha chuckled. "Deal."

The house was quiet for a few minutes. She knew it wouldn't last. The movie crew came and went constantly. They were paying her quite well for the weeks they'd be there. It ensured a great nest egg for when she opened to the public. They'd even offered her extra for the possibility of shooting a scene in the garden. Tesha went to her office. She'd yet to sign the final contract to give to the movie executives as they kept changing and adding things. Not a big problem since each time they offered more money, but she'd feel better with at least one signed copy.

She looked to the corner of her office at Kylie's bed and pouted. She missed the little bundle of fur. But for the time being, Mrs. Miller had taken her to keep her out of the way. "Four weeks, Tesh, and then life will return to normal," she told herself out loud.

Normal. What exactly was that? Her website was going up that week. Cleve had it prepped and ready and was just waiting for her to give the go ahead. Once that was done, she'd begin taking reservations. So far with the current guests, everything was going almost perfectly.

The only glitch was the bathroom situation upstairs. She'd not planned for men and women to share a bathroom unless they were a couple, and one of the pampered actors announced his intention to move out. He changed his tune upon realizing the only other accommodations were a motel in town or the trailer on the property.

Several RVs were parked across the street on Mr. Moore's land, to his delight of course. He'd already invited her to several parties for the cast and crew. The evening before, she saw the camera crew and other movie workers on the wraparound porch, seeming quite at home.

She felt his presence before seeing him. Her skin prickled and her idiot heart skipped a beat. "Tesha?"

Adam was just outside the door. It took her a minute to compose herself enough to reply. "I'm in here."

Do not act stupid. Don't let him see how he affects you. "Stop it," Tesha grumbled at her stupid butterfly filled stomach.

He walked to the doorway and stopped, his eyes locking with hers. "Hi."

There was something in that one little word that spoke volumes. Adam rarely spoke much before, not with words anyway. She'd learned he said more with facial expressions and his eyes than words. Right now they told her he needed a friend. The last thing she wanted was another ex-lover as a friend. Especially not the man who turned her entire body into a mess of goo and shivers so she remained sitting. "Hi."

He took a deep breath as if it took a lot to talk. "My house is a mess."

She'd wondered why he'd agreed to the movie. It didn't seem like something a loner like him would do. "There certainly have been a lot of changes in two days. So many people all over the place. And they cut the trees on the other side."

He nodded. "They took down my dog pen." His shoulders slumped and Tesha couldn't hold back anymore. She stood and went to him. She wrapped her arms around his waist. Her heart went out to him when he exhaled and his arms surrounded her, his head resting on top of hers.

They stood like that for a long time, his strong heartbeat

thudding under her ear, the solid body against hers.

"Why did you agree to the movie?" Tesha did not move away. She was so mad at him for dating, wanted an explanation all the while knowing she had no right to ask, especially since she'd done the same. Gone on a dinner date with James Malloy.

"I didn't. Jensen did what Jensen always does. He means well, thinks he's doing me a favor by showcasing the house and throwing money at me."

It was heartwarming to see how in spite of how angry he must be at his brother, Adam still justified Jensen's actions. Obviously the strong tie of being family meant he'd forgive the actor. "You have furniture now." Tesha pushed away reluctantly and smiled up at him. "That's something."

He didn't reply, his eyes locked on her lips.

Tesha swallowed. He was going to kiss her and she needed to stop it. Move away. She didn't move an inch.

His lips were familiar, erotic, and delicious covering hers. His tongue prodded for entrance and she opened her mouth allowing him full access. His large body shielded her from the outside world and for a moment, the cocoon of them together erased all the stress of the day.

When his hands slid down her back and cupped her bottom to pull her against him, Tesha moaned at the wonderful friction of the bulge beneath his jeans and her light cotton dress. He deepened the kiss conveying hunger and need. God she wanted him.

"Whoa," Jensen's voice permeated through the fog of desire. Tesha jumped back and Adam growled.

"Sorry to interrupt." By Jensen's broad smile, he was not in the least sorry. His rounded eyes looked from her to Adam. "I didn't know you two were that cozy."

"Shut up." Adam moved behind Tesha and put his hands on her shoulders. She figured he needed a few minutes for his arousal to deflate, but unfortunately that placed her flushed face, crinkled dress and mused hair front and center.

Jensen's gaze traveled over her until Adam grunted, "What do you want?"

"Came to talk to you. Saw your truck out front," Jensen replied and took a bite of an apple he'd been holding. "Actually," he looked to Tesha's desk. "I also wanted to see you. Can I look at the contract?"

He strolled past them and glanced down at the papers she'd been holding earlier.

Tesha moved away from Adam suddenly feeling awkward. She was not happy with him and the sooner her treacherous body got with the program, the better. Once Jensen left, she'd explain to Adam they would be friends only. No sex, no making out in doorways. He'd understand the difference between chemistry and a relationship. She didn't want the no strings attached arrangement with him anymore. It wouldn't work now that her feelings for him had changed.

Adam sat and scowled at his brother. She noticed a light bruise on his temple and joined him in the glare at Jensen.

The actor's entire disposition changed, in that moment she saw the less playful carefree facade fall. Jensen looked at his brother accessing the scowl and then looked worried. "How are you today? Were you all right last night when you went home?"

Ah yes, the PTSD.

Adam nodded. "The only dream I had was of stomping your pea brain into the ground."

Jensen grinned and Adam rolled his eyes. "What do you want to talk about?"

"First this," Jensen said while scribbling on the contract and with flourish placing an 'X' where Tesha should sign. "I fixed the numbers."

Tesha moved closer and glanced at the paper. He'd doubled some of the figures and adjusted others. "Are you sure?"

"Yep," Jensen replied. "Trust me, they are offering a pittance compared to the other sites. They figured you wouldn't know better. Besides, you've got them by the balls. The location is set."

Tesha took the pen and signed it. "I'll go and drop this off. Give you two privacy to talk."

"We need to talk too." Adam told her, the scowl still firmly in place, but his eyes softened when meeting hers. "Please."

"Okay. Sure, later. Right now, I have to get things ready for the afternoon meal."

Chapter Twenty-One

ADAM WAS TORN between relief his brother had interrupted his attempt to seduce Tesha and making a stupid mistake and wanting to pound the brat into a pulp for ruining the wonderful moment. He didn't want Tesha to be just a sex-only arrangement. He wanted more. At the same time, he wasn't sure how she felt about him. Sure she responded to his touch, but that didn't mean she accepted him fully.

Doctor Mitchell told him it would take time before Adam could presume to be well enough to be in a relationship with someone. Needed more time in order for the doctor to be assured Adam could be trusted to live at close quarters and not possibly hurt the person.

If he ever injured Tesha, he would not forgive himself. The damn tug of war between what he should do: walk away and let her move on, or do what he wanted—make her his.

"I'm sorry." Jensen interrupted his musings. "Mom called me yesterday and tore me a new asshole about all this." He motioned to the door in the direction of Adam's house. "I should have thought about what effect all of this could have on your recovery."

"Fuck my recovery, Jensen, what about my house, the property. That's what pisses me off."

"Yeah, well, you'll be surprised how much nicer it will look once it's done."

"I have a fucking restaurant for a backyard." Adam held back ensuring not to scream in case Tesha was within earshot.

"It's more like a bistro. With that fancy outdoor grill, you and Tesha can have some awesome parties." Jensen wiggled his brows. "I bet she agrees with me."

"Tesha and I are just…"

"Yeah right, just friends…I have those kind of friends, too." Jensen chuckled and bit into his apple. "She's hot."

"Don't look at her." Adam's voice as low and hoarse as he leaned forward. "I mean it, Jensen, don't even look at her."

"Oh shit." Jensen let out a whistle. "It's that serious?"

"Drop it." Adam stood. He needed to go to the house and get clothes. Then he'd look for Tesha and talk to her. About what, he wasn't sure yet.

He stepped outside Tesha's office door and came to an abrupt stop. Vanessa Morgan stood beside the kitchen counter. She placed the glass she had in her hand on the counter and her lips curved up at seeing him. Behind her, Tesha was busy doing something. She'd not noticed he'd walked out of the office.

He looked to the doorway needing to escape what could possibly ruin any chance with Tesha. He and Vanessa had met before, at a party when he'd visited Jensen in Hollywood not too long after returning from Afghanistan. They'd had a one night, or make that a two night stand which had become ingrained in his mind for a long time. The woman was a lusty lover who took no prisoners. In those two nights, she'd taught him things he'd not even known existed.

"Hey, lover," she crooned.

Shit.

Tesha's head popped up and she looked to him and then to Vanessa. The actress stepped toward him, an air of expectancy about her. "What an unexpected turn of events. Just when I thought I'd die of boredom. Here you are."

Adam's throat went dry, he didn't dare look at Tesha who watched them, not moving.

Just as Vanessa closed in, Jensen stepped between them and took the actress by the shoulders. "Stop teasing my brother. You know how conservative he is. Hell, he was a virgin until his late twenties." Jensen tugged the confused Vanessa towards the French doors. "We thought he was going to be a priest until finally dad hired a hooker to take care of popping that cherry," Jensen continued.

"What?" Vanessa tried in vain to turn back to Adam. "I didn't need to know that, did I?"

They went outside and Jensen slammed the door firmly behind them.

"That was a lame attempt to keep me from figuring out you and her had something once." Tesha had her fists on her hips and gave him a droll look. "It's none of my business what you did or do. As a matter of fact. I needed a moment to tell you we need to cool things. I don't think it's a good idea…" she stopped talking when he walked around the kitchen counter and stood close to her. Definitely invading her personal space. She blinked. "We don't have any kind of commitment so it doesn't matter who you date."

"Is this because you're dating Malloy?"

"Who? Oh, James."

"Yes, oh James. He told me you and him are keeping in

touch." Adam hated how he couldn't keep the jealous anger from his voice. "You got my dog." He looked around the room for the first time noticing he'd not seen the puppy. "Where's my dog?"

"She's mine now, he said I could have her. Never once have you even asked about her or came for her. You just assumed everything would remain the same. That Kylie would be right here waiting. That all you had to do was show up one day and she'd be yours without you having to explain anything or do more than crook your finger."

She wasn't talking about the dog anymore. Guilt at the truth in her words made him take a step backward. "I'm sorry, you're right."

A tear trailed down her cheek and she brushed it away with a quick swipe. "I'm really busy, Adam. I have to fix lunch for the movie crew."

"I thought the people behind my house did that."

"They do dinner. I am responsible for breakfast and lunch for fifteen people." She picked up the knife and began chopping carrots. "Please go." Her sniff made his chest constrict.

"I want more between us." He stepped closer.

The door opened and two men walked in. One neared the counter and settled into a barstool. "I need coffee. Strong black."

Tesha poured him a cup. "I signed the new copy of the contract. Let me get it," she told one of the men and moved around Adam to rush into her office.

The man sized him up. "I hear you're good at stunts."

Adam groaned and left.

Chapter Twenty-Two

TESHA COULDN'T BELIEVE how fast the days flew by since they'd taken on the catering work for the movie production. She'd barely had time to get a shower and collapse into bed before it was time to get back up and straight to preparation for the breakfast meal.

She'd not seen Adam and although she didn't ask, Jensen volunteered that Adam was back to working with their older brother at Ford Enterprises. Although it had intrigued her, she'd not asked what Tristan was like. The handsome man seemed rather intimidating and aloof.

Mrs. Miller and her energetic duo of Debbie and Carol burst into the room with trays of empty glasses. "Everyone loved the sweet tea," Mrs. Miller announced and placed the tray carefully on the counter. "Carol almost dropped her pitcher when she saw Liam Neeson was here."

"I swear I almost fainted," Ms. Carol agreed. "My stars, I've never seen so many famous people."

Tesha laughed when the woman sat and fanned her heated face. "I don't know that I'll ever get used to it."

The women had shown up the day before offering to help when news more movie stars had arrived, and a grateful Tesha hired them on the spot to serve the afternoon meal. The Hollywood types were demanding and driving her and Cassie crazy with constant demands. Thankfully, she'd learned to say no pretty quick. Cassie was still working on it.

Tesha began premixing the ingredients for the ham and cheese biscuits for the next morning. The dough would sit in the refrigerator overnight. Although she planned to only serve them a couple times a week, the execs had amended the contract, giving her even more money, to serve them daily. Tesha smiled when the trio of women ran to the windows and peered towards the trailers parked across the way. "Is that Matt Damon?" Mrs. Miller exclaimed.

Tesha peered over their shoulders. "No, that's a cameraman."

"Well, he certainly could double for Matt Damon," Mrs. Miller insisted. She turned and went back to the kitchen. "Let's clean up, ladies. I suggest we then take a long break on the front porch and drink some of the delicious sweet tea before heading home."

"It's a wonderful idea." The other two immediately agreed and before long, were ensconced in the rockers on the porch, tall glasses in hand.

Tesha's cell phone rang. She was waiting on a call from Cassie so without looking at the display she hit the answer button.

"Tesha?" It was Adam and of course her ridiculous stomach immediately flipped and flopped.

"Hello, Adam. I'm pretty busy..."

He cleared his throat. "I know. I tried to catch you before I left, but was told you'd gone into town. I went to town, but didn't see you there."

"I went to Nashville." She wondered what the purpose of

his call was. At least this time before leaving, he'd tried to say goodbye.

"We need to talk." The last thing she wanted right now was a conversation with Adam. The distraction of the conflicting emotions when it came to him confused her too much.

"Now?"

"No, I'm coming there tomorrow. Can I stay at your house?"

In her room? Was that his real question? "I don't have any spare beds." She swallowed in spite of the fact he couldn't see her.

"Does that mean no?" It sounded as if he teased her.

Tesha chuckled. "It means there are no extra beds. I have a couch."

There was a moment of silence. "I'll kick Jensen out of my room, he can sleep on the floor or in the trailer or come here to Nashville. He said they weren't shooting tomorrow."

She'd planned a day home alone, since the actress and other guests had announced they were spending the weekend in Nashville. Now, she wondered how relaxing it would be, knowing Adam would be coming. Especially since they'd not discussed his date with the blonde.

That night, she lay in bed and stared at the ceiling. Kylie slept next to her, the puppy was ecstatic when she'd plopped her on the bed, next to her. Sure it was a bad habit to start, but it could be a good obstacle to keep Adam out. She picked up the cell phone and considered texting him. Maybe if she sent a message telling him they would only remain friendly neighbors and nothing more, he wouldn't come expecting an easy tryst.

He'd not been hesitant to ask to spend the night, knowing full well most of the cast was going to be in Nashville. There were probably plenty of empty beds at his house.

Tesha huffed and flopped onto her stomach. Why did this have to happen? The hurdle of her feelings for Adam was making sleep impossible.

Along with bright sunshine, the birds outside were cheerful and loud. Tesha glared at the window and wondered what the hell they were so damn happy about. She'd finally fallen asleep around three in the morning, and now the little chirpers woke her up.

Kylie shook and inched closer. She licked Tesha's cheek. "Okay, I'm up. I'm awake." She trudged to the side door and let the puppy out. "So much for sleeping in." She scratched her head and stare bleary-eyed at the clock on the microwave. It was nine-thirty. She'd actually slept in, it didn't feel like it. Where was everyone? The noise in the kitchen should have woken her when Cassie arrived to cook. She went to the French doors and peered out.

In a grassy area between the houses, there was a small tent erected. Under it, tables and chairs. A van with bright red letters was parked on the street, "Red's Pancake House" in large red letters on its side.

Cassie walked into the garden, saw her and waved. She had a plate piled with pancakes and slipped in to the house. "Isn't it great? They showed up at the same time I did and offered to feed the crew free of charge. I looked in on you and you were passed out, so I didn't wake you. I stole your phone so it wouldn't wake you either." She pointed to Tesha's phone on the counter.

"I didn't hear anything. The birds woke me up." Tesha slumped into a chair and dug into the pancakes Cassie slid in front of her. "I hope the execs don't decide to hire them instead of us."

"They can't, we have a contract," Cassie replied between bites. "Besides, they are from Nashville and came for today only. Some sort of publicity stunt I'm sure. These are good."

"Hmpf," Tesha reached for the cup of coffee that magically appeared. She guessed Cassie had poured it when she'd had her face inches from the pancakes.

"You don't look good." Cassie narrowed her eyes. "Are you sick?"

"Nope, just tired. Restless night."

"Worried about something?"

"Adam is coming to 'talk.'" She made quotation mark motions with her fingers. "It shouldn't worry me so much, I mean, what can he possibly have to talk about? He assumes we're friends with benefits. Maybe he's bringing the woman he went out with to live with him and wants to warn me. Or maybe he wants to continue to be friends with benefits and wants to date other women in Nashville."

"Oh." Cassie frowned. "What if he wants to take your relationship to the next level?"

"No friends, just benefits?"

Cassie let out a giggle. "No silly, monogamy."

"I doubt that very much," Tesha grumbled. "I don't think he's the boyfriend type. I don't want to be his girlfriend. We're better off as friends."

"You're about to find out, he just walked up to the gate."

"Oh shit." Tesha shot up to her feet and ran toward her bedroom. "Stop him. I'm not ready. I look like crap."

"Says the girl who just wants to be friends," Cassie called out after her.

Chapter Twenty-Three

Adam caught sight of Tesha's pajama clad bottom as she raced to her bedroom and slammed the door shut behind her. Her friend, Cassie, sat at the dining table with a cup of coffee up to her smiling face, eyes trained on him.

Her gaze followed him as he walked into the room, but she didn't say anything until he sat down. "Tesha wants me to stop you from going to her bedroom. She's not ready."

"Not ready for what?"

She shrugged. "I don't know exactly. I think she needs to change or something."

Adam considered going to Tesha's bedroom, but decided to respect her wishes, so instead he slid the plate she'd left closer and began to eat.

"I'll be on my way, since we didn't have to cook lunch today, it gives me a chance to go to the store." Cassie stood and grabbed her purse. "Don't do anything dumb. She's a great person and deserves to be treated well."

"I'll try my best. She is and you're right."

His answer seemed to appease the pretty woman who gave him a bright smile. Her smile disappeared and was replaced with a gawk when his brother walked in through the doors.

"Hey," Jensen said to both of them, then smiled at Cassie, who whirled and rushed from the room and out the front door.

"That makes two women who ran away when seeing one of us," Adam told Jensen. "Tesha ran to her room when I walked in and now you scared off Cassie."

"She's cute," Jensen said and pulled back the chair Cassie had just vacated. "I think she likes me."

"Most women do," Adam replied not liking that Jensen might take advantage of the sweet woman. "You should steer clear of her. She's not the play with kind."

"I know," Jensen replied surprising him. "That's why I haven't tried anything."

"Sometimes you surprise me." Adam studied his younger brother. With hazel and dark blond hair like Tristan's, he seemed at ease. Jensen always wore his hair a bit longer than he and his brothers, touching his collar and cut in a style that somehow looked messy yet perfect at the same time. As usual when not working, he wore his favorite color, black t-shirt shirt and black jeans. Beneath the sleeve on his left arm, the bottom of his tribal tattoo peaked out.

Jensen stretched. "I'm not going to Nashville with the crew. Selene is coming to spend a couple nights."

"Where is she staying?" Adam bristled. His plans to stay in his house suddenly complicated.

"In my room. Well, your room, but mine for now." Jensen smiled. "I got some special sheets and fancy bedding all set. You can keep them after I leave."

"Yuck."

"Duh, they'll get laundered." Jensen stood. "See ya later, bro."

"I was planning to stay here this weekend." Adam stood

and glared at his brother. "I need my bedroom."

"No can do." Jensen skirted around him and left.

Adam turned to watch Jensen walk through the garden and on to his house. "What an ass."

"Who?" Tesha stood behind him.

"Jensen just kicked me out of my own house. He's an idiot if he thinks I'm not going back in."

She looked fresh and beautiful in a pair of denim shorts and a light green gauzy top. She didn't wear much makeup as usual, her lips only slightly colored with a soft shimmer. He noted she'd cut her hair recently and it was styled in the cute pixie cut she'd worn when first arriving.

Her large brown eyes searched his face. Once again wariness in her expression. "He's a character."

It was time to let down his guard, to open himself to her and hope for a good outcome. In the best of times, he wasn't good at communicating. Now he prayed the right words would come. He took her hand and pulled her toward the table. "Please, sit."

"If I have to sit for this, I'm not sure I want to." Tesha resisted only a bit. "How about we go to the front porch? I need fresh air."

They made their way to the front of the house. He couldn't keep his eyes off her delicious body. The thought of her soft skin against him dried his throat. Tesha was beautiful, exotic, tantalizing. He wanted her more than ever.

Before she could take a seat, he wrapped an arm around her waist and kissed her shoulder. "I miss you. Miss being your neighbor."

THE HUSKINESS IN Adam's voice made Tesha shudder. This was the time to be strong. She couldn't let his sweet words or enticing body woo her into doing something stupid. Tesha moved away from him and leaned on the railing. "What is so important that you couldn't tell me over the phone? I don't want you to touch me until we talk, clear things up. I can't think when you are too close."

She took a fortifying breath when he hung his head and looked at his feet. "You're not making this easy."

Here it came the "I'm seeing someone else speech." Or better yet, "I want to remain lovers, but only when I come here on weekends," proposal.

When he lifted his head and looked at her, she almost gasped. His heavily lashed eyes were dark, the blue almost turquoise in color. So beautiful. The corner of his sensual mouth lifted. "I am not ready for a relationship. That's what my therapist says. That I should take things slow and wait until I have better control over my flashbacks."

"Of course, I understand. No problem." Tesha wanted to run back inside and lock the door. Instead, she ran her finger along the top of the railing and then stopped when she noticed it shook with restrained annoyance. "He probably also suggested you date and enjoy being a bachelor."

"Yes, he did actually." Adam neared, the warmth of his breath on the side of her face made her eyes close. "But I don't want to."

"Adam." She couldn't move away. At this moment she hated how much he affected her. "What do you want me to do? I don't know that I can be just friends, but also I can't continue to be more than that. It's hard for me to keep my heart from getting involved."

"I—I want to ask you to give me a chance. I realize I'm asking a lot. That man you saw that night is still inside me. But I don't want to lose you. Will you give me a chance, Tesha? Give a relationship between us a try?"

Tesha blinked and her mouth opened. What exactly had he just asked? "Do you mean you want a relationship with me?"

He nodded. "Yes."

"Oh." Now it was her who found it hard to speak. "I'm not sure what to think. You just threw a curveball at me."

"I understand if you need time to think." His shoulders slumped slightly, before he straightened in an attempt to look unaffected. But she'd seen the hurt in his eyes when thinking she would turn him down.

"I don't have to think about it, Adam." Tesha smiled and took his right hand in both of hers. "I don't want to lose you either."

"Is that a yes?"

Her heart melted at the expectation in his expression. His eyebrows high, his rounded eyes locked with hers. Could it be possible that this amazing man was actually in love, or more realistically, in like, with her?

"It's a yes." Before she could say anything else, she was engulfed in his arms, his mouth searched for hers and she lifted her face to him. He tasted of coffee, pancake syrup, and possibilities.

Her fingers weaved through his soft hair as she allowed him to deepen the kiss, and his hands, flat on her back, held her flush against her.

The warmth of his kiss sent her heart fluttering, her

breathing becoming more like pants when his lips traveled down from her jawline to the side of Tesha's neck. She'd missed him so much. Longed for his touches and caresses. It was a strange feeling to know she could allow herself the luxury of enjoying him and make plans with him. Her scrambled mind came to a screeching stop when the picture of him kissing the woman's hand in the restaurant popped front and center of her mind. How could she have forgotten that?

Tesha pushed away and looked up at him. It took a moment to see clearly past the fog of wanting to drag him back inside for a leisurely morning in bed. "What about that woman you went out with? Do you plan to see her again?"

"Never. It was a business dinner. She propositioned me and I said no. I couldn't when I thought of how it would affect us…you." Adam's brows were drawn down over his eyes. "What about Malloy?"

"We only went out once, and we've not spoken in weeks. I have not seen him since."

"You're expecting me to tell you I won't see anyone else," Adam stated the obvious matter-of-factly. "I won't see anyone else. I hope you won't either. I want us to be exclusive."

"Good."

Tesha smiled up at him, she tugged at his hand. "I planned to go into town today and pick up groceries and then maybe go for a drive and relax. Would you like to do that with me?"

He smiled and for the first time she saw a flash of what he must have looked like when he was carefree and didn't carry the burdens of a war on his shoulders. "Sure."

She was happy he'd not pushed her for more right then. It was best they ease into things, spend the day together and get used to the idea of being in a relationship. Although admittedly it would have not taken much effort to convince her otherwise, it meant a lot that he was fine with spending time doing mundane things.

A few minutes later, she sat beside Adam in his truck. He drove along a two-lane highway. The radio was set to classic rock the windows down letting the warm air in. Tesha couldn't help stealing sideways glances at him. He wore aviator sunglasses and a navy blue polo shirt. His jeans were worn and fit him perfectly. He was an amazing looking guy.

She reached over and slid her fingers down the side of his face. "Pull over."

"Is something wrong?" He searched her face and then his eyes widened in surprise when she slid her other hand to his thigh and between his legs.

"Yes, something is terribly wrong. I want you."

He looked into the rear view mirror and then to her. "Someone could drive up."

"I know. But I don't think they will stop." Tesha leaned over and ran the tip of her tongue along his ear lobe. "I can't wait."

Adam pulled the truck off the road and drove up a bumpy gravel path and pulled to a stop. Tesha yelped and giggled when he grabbed her and pulled her over him.

His mouth was hungry when it took hers and his hands were already under her shirt unfastening her bra. When her breasts fell free he yanked her top off and took her nipple into his mouth to suckle. Tesha almost came then and there. She struggled to pull her shorts off and finally was able to after much maneuvering. Being completely nude while Adam remained dressed was erotic as all get out.

His eyes raked over her in appreciation. "Damn you're incredible. So beautiful."

He moaned when she reached between them and caressed his thick arousal. "Damn, Tesh, I can't wait to be inside you."

"Me, either. I need you now." She unzipped him and shoved his fly open then pushed his briefs down to release his erection. It jutted straight up, hard and enticing. As much as she wanted it between her lips, there wasn't time. She straddled him and lowered, taking him in.

Adam held her hips and his own jutted up until he thrust his entire length into her.

"Oh God!" Tesha cried out, her body trembling. "Oh!"

"Ride me." His command stirred her into action and she placed her hands on his shoulders and did just that.

The combination of being in the confined space of a truck, out where they could be discovered and his happy grunts brought Tesha to a quick orgasm.

The sounds of their bodies meeting brought her to start a second climb.

Adam let out a deeper moan and grabbed her hips lifting and lowering her. His moved faster, the thrusts harder. "Oh shit," he panted in her ear. "I'm about to lose it. You probably should get off me."

Before she could move, he lost control. His body took over, grabbing her hips and holding her in place. Adam began to tremble, threw his head back, cried out and came.

It was then she realized they were not using protection. Tesha couldn't budge. He held her fast, his hot release filling her. She shook as she too succumbed to an orgasm that had her shaking from head to toe. She collapsed against his chest while he peppered kisses on her temples and face.

"Damn, Tesh. I didn't mean to come inside you. Are you mad?" He lifted her face and his soft gaze met hers. "I assure you, I'm clean."

"No, of course I'm not mad." She pressed a kiss to the tip of his nose. "But I am going to stress out until my period comes. I'm not taking any birth control."

She waited for the panic. For him to scramble to separate and begin to babble. Instead he wrapped his arms around her and held her. "I know we're not ready for anything that drastic. But I want kids, I would love it if you get pregnant."

"Seriously, Adam." Tesha gave him a droll look. "I'm adding pharmacy to our stops." She let out a breath and scanned the view of the road through the back window. "We probably should go before cops show up or something."

It took a while for her to get dressed, especially since she had to keep brushing Adam's hands away.

Once she dressed and they were on their way, Tesha bit her bottom lip.

"You're worried." Adam slid his eyes to her. "I'm sure you're not pregnant."

Tesha let out a chuckle. "You can't be sure of that. I'm fine. I'll make an appointment first thing on Monday to get birth control."

His hands slid down her arm and took her hand. "I meant what I said. If something comes of it. I will marry you immediately."

Although her heart warmed at the thought he'd stand by her, Tesha hoped that wouldn't be the only reason he'd offer marriage.

God how she hoped there wouldn't be a consequence to making the maddeningly delicious man pull over.

Yes, that was exactly how she felt in spite of the smile tugging at her lips.

Chapter Twenty-Four

THREE DAYS LATER, Adam hung up after speaking to Tesha. He sat back in his leather executive chair and looked out the window. Her period had started. She sounded relieved and laughed when he'd told her he was already making a list of names. He wasn't kidding.

When she told him she'd gotten birth control and they didn't have to use condoms anymore, Adam was somewhat appeased.

He planned to marry Tesha, but knew it would take a little time before she'd accept. And there was the matter with Doctor Mitchell. The doc wouldn't be pleased when he found out he'd went ahead with a relationship. Which reminded him. He had a call to make.

It was time to make it clear to Malloy he wouldn't appreciate the guy calling Tesha anymore. He grimaced at his need to be overly aggressive. If Tesha found out he was making calls that made him more caveman than anything else, she'd be mad. Okay, he'd call Malloy and insure the guy understood he and Tesha were in a committed relationship. He would do his best not to growl or threaten.

"I CAN'T BELIEVE you called James." Tesha's voice was raised an octave in his ear. "It wasn't your call to make. I planned to tell him if he ever called again."

"Well, he obviously called."

Adam made a mental note to pound the guy into the ground if he ever saw him again.

"Yes, he called, I left him a message about Kylie's papers." Tesha huffed. "You can't go all barbarian on me, Adam. I have male friends and I am not the kind of girl who will sit back and let you club them over the head. Cleve for instance."

"Is he more than a friend?"

"Ugh!" Tesha hung up.

Adam sat back with a smirk. She loved him. Then he sat forward. Or did she just kick him to the curb. He picked up the cell phone and called her back.

"Yes, Adam." She didn't sound mad. "I'm busy, it's almost time to serve lunch."

"I'm sorry."

"Just so you understand. I know we have to get to know more about each other and it will take some time. But I'm telling you right now. You cannot threaten any person who happens to be male who I talk to."

"Understood." He couldn't help it sounded more like a growl.

"See you Friday night." She made a kiss sound and hung up.

Flashes of lights blinded him. Adam ducked behind something, what it was didn't matter. What mattered was that he was back. The sounds of crossfire and helicopter blades thudded and cracked. His hands trembled, but he managed to clutch to the fabric of the injured man's uniform. Whoever he dragged was heavy. It proved impossible to pull him to safety behind the barrier. He tugged and heaved, his heart pounding. Then the soldier was gone.

The helicopter blades became distant and he screamed in panic. They were leaving him behind. His hands were red with blood when he looked down to look for a weapon. There was only blood. So much blood.

Blind, Adam scrambled from his bed and crawled to the corner of the bedroom. He hugged his knees to his chest and began to rock forward and backward. They'd be coming to get him, kill him. He'd failed his mission.

Chapter Twenty-Five

TESHA CHECKED THROUGH the window once again. Other than a motorcycle, which she knew belonged to Jensen and another convertible, which she assumed was Jensen's guest there were no other new vehicles. Lights blazed from the other side of the house. They were filming. It was almost ten o'clock at night and they were still working.

Once the shooting was done, Vanessa Morgan and the other two actors who were staying at her house would trudge in and after picking at some snacks, they'd go to bed.

Her cell phone had been silent all evening, no news from Adam. No call, text, or message. She'd called and sent him a text to see if he was all right, but he'd not answered. Each time she imagined the worst, that he'd been in an accident between Nashville and Lovely, she was reassured since Jensen was not notified. The actor would not hesitate to come and inform her.

The oven timer dinged and she checked the last batch of snicker doodles. Most of the actors didn't eat more than raw vegetables, but the rest of the crew would appreciate a warm cookie or two before bed.

The kitchen filled with the cinnamon aroma of the cookies as she slid each one onto a cooling rack. She sent a third text asking if he was on his way.

No reply came.

Once the cookies were put up, she'd shower and go to bed. In the morning Adam would arrive and explain the reason for his not coming as planned.

"You don't look good at all." The next afternoon Cassie studied Tesha, who ignored her and continued to scrub the baking pan. "Have you slept?"

Tesha blew out a breath and slid a look to the two execs in her kitchen, paperwork and all sort of other office supplies scattered across the long dining room table. "I did not sleep well. Have a lot on my mind." She wiped her hands on her apron. "As a matter of fact. Would you mind finishing up alone? I need to go over to the other house."

The expression on Cassie's face relaxed. "Sure."

Jensen sat on a new couch, his head bopping along with whatever music he listened too. When Tesha signaled that she wanted to talk to him. He pulled the headset off and stood. "What's up?"

Other than two men in the kitchen staring bleakly into their cups of coffee, there was no one else around. Tesha wondered if they were filming a portion that did not require Jensen at the moment. "I feel silly coming to you about this, but I'm worried about Adam. He planned to come this weekend, but hasn't."

Jensen frowned and pulled out his cell phone from his back pocket. "I got a couple texts from Caden, but haven't had a chance to read them." He held up a finger. "Hold on."

His eyes widened. "Damn."

"What?" Tesha's heart lodged in the vicinity of her throat.

"He says he wrecked the Porsche again."

Her voice made a strangled sound. "Adam?"

Jensen looked up at her as if he'd forgotten she was there. "No, Caden. I'm going to kick his ass."

Tesha wanted to kick him in the knee. "What about Adam?"

"I have no idea. Let me call." For a few minutes Jensen walked in a circle, one hand on his hip while saying a lot of "uh-huh's" and "okay's." Finally he hung up and turned to her. "Adam's in the hospital. A clinic. He didn't want anyone to call you and tell you. So I'm not supposed to tell you."

"Where is he?" Tesha asked through clenched teeth.

"Cornerstone," Jensen replied with rounded eyes. The actor would never make a good spy in real life. He folded rather easily when faced with an angry woman.

Through the red haze of fury, Tesha began checking things off her mental to do list. Breakfast items were cleared off. Lunch items prepared and ready to be set out. Mrs. Miller, Carol, and Debbie were due at any minute to serve it. She had plenty of time for murder.

Cassie was sliding her large tote onto her shoulder when Tesha walked back into her house. "I have dash to my shop," Cassie said holding up her car keys. "I have four dozen cupcakes to decorate and deliver for a ladies' tea two towns over." Her wide eyes took in Tesha's scowl. "What are you doing today?"

"I'm going to Nashville to kill Adam. Maybe stop on the way back and pick up ten gallons of butter pecan ice cream."

"Oh." Cassie seemed at a loss as to whether to believe her or not. "Do you need an accomplice?"

Tesha chuckled in spite of her sour humor. "You're a great

friend. Thanks for the offer, but this is a one-woman job. I'll call you later."

Somewhat mollified, Cassie left. Tesha changed from her stained kitchen smock to a clingy white t-shirt with the words "I Love Pink" in bright pink letters and the emblem of a heart on the front.

An hour later she motored her small truck to the clinic in Nashville.

Cornerstone Treatment Center was a midsize nondescript one story building flanked by a parking lot and what looked to be a fenced in park. The trees behind it were tall, shading part of the clinic's roof. Tesha pushed the heavy door open and stepped into a cheery front room. A young receptionist looked up from her monitor and smiled. "Good afternoon. How can I help you?"

"I'm here to see Adam Ford," Tesha didn't smile back. Her mood had gotten worse instead of better on the drive. How dare Adam keep this from her, leave her high and dry after making plans to spend their first weekend as a couple together. Above all, why would he tell his family to keep it from her? It angered her that he expected her to be on some sort of permanent stand-by.

The woman typed something into a computer and looked up at her. "Name?"

"Tesha Washington."

She looked to her monitor and back at her. "Mr. Ford has a green light. He's in Room 14. Down the hall on your left," the woman told her already looking back to her monitor. "Please knock softly a couple times first. Some of our patients need a warning before someone enters."

Green light? Tesha looked down the hallway. Every doorway had a shingle type display with lights. Most were green, a few were red.

Upon approaching the doorway, Tesha hesitated. What if his family was in there? They were not at the "meet the parents" stage yet.

She rapped twice on the door. No answer. She pushed the door open just a bit and peeked in. Adam was asleep. His wrists and ankles were bound with what looked to be leather bindings. A gasp escaped from her throat. If she was angry before, now she was enraged. How dare they do this to him?

He woke up when she was working on the second wrist. His free hand stopped her. "You can't do that." Adam's words were a bit slurred, she wondered if they'd drugged him.

"I can and I will. How could your family allow this?"

"I don't want to hurt you." Adam seemed to struggle to keep his eyes open. He studied her face. "Why are you here?"

She shoved his hand aside and finished releasing his wrist. "Why did you tell your family not to contact me?"

He looked away from her to the wall. "Go home, Tesha. It was a mistake. I can't be in a relationship. I'm still a mess."

Her rage immediately receded at the fat tear that slipped from the corner of his eye, down the side of his face and dripped to the pillow.

"Please, leave." His voice was softer. His head lolled to the side.

"He'll be out for a while. I ordered a sedative to keep him from struggling against the bonds." A doctor spoke matter-of-factly from the doorway. "Doctor Mitchell." The physician came toward her and held out his hand. "I assume you're his

Tesha."

His. "I'm not so sure I'm 'his' anything right now." She held Adam's hand, couldn't release it. She'd never seen so much pain, what she'd seen in Adam's eyes would stay with her for a long time. "What happened?"

Doctor Mitchell eyed the unfastened restraint, but didn't move to restrain Adam's wrist again. "He had a pretty bad episode. His family couldn't get him to snap out of it, so they called me."

Adam looked so strong, virile, and heartbreakingly handsome in his slumber. A lock of hair across his drawn brows, his full lips slightly parted. Tesha faced the doctor. "I should leave."

"No, it may do him some good that you're here. I don't suggest you listen to anything he says while drugged. Although I don't recommend patients undergoing PTSD counseling to enter into a relationship, I think losing you would affect him negatively at this point."

"Do you know what brought this on?"

Doctor Mitchell's smile came across as fatherly. "If I did I couldn't tell you. But no, I don't know. Sometimes a certain memory will trigger them. Other times, they just happen without a reason."

The doctor made a note on the clipboard. "If you need anything push that button." He motioned to a round-lighted button on the wall with the words "Assistance Needed" in bold letters under it.

Tesha moved to sit in an overstuffed chair in the corner of Adam's room. She checked emails and played a game on her cell phone for several hours.

A couple walked in. They looked to be in their early fifties. The woman had beautiful grey hair, cut in a stylish bob. The man, clearly a Ford with dark salt and pepper hair and blue eyes had his hand in the small of the woman's back.

"Hello," the woman went to Tesha after looking at the still slumbering Adam. "I'm Miriam, Adam's mother." She smiled at Tesha with obvious curiosity.

Tesha stood, oh boy, she'd not meant to meet them yet. She smiled back. "I'm Tesha Washington. His…"

"Oh yes, Jensen told us all about you. You're the girl Adam is seeing."

She meant to say, his neighbor.

"Jensen talks too much," Adam grunted from the bed, having woken at hearing his parents enter. His sullen gaze tracked the people in the room.

The older man nodded at Tesha, his eyes warm. "I'm Roman Ford, the patient's father."

"Dad…" Adam groaned and put his hands over his eyes. "My head hurts. The lights are too bright."

Mariam Ford, moved with brisk efficiency. She lit the lamp next to Adam's bed and then flicked off the room lights. "There, now we can get to know your girl. We've not heard much about you yet." She reached out and patted Tesha's shoulder. "It's wonderful to meet you, Tesha. I'm glad to know you are giving our son a chance."

At once she felt at ease. She'd wondered at their reaction upon meeting Adam's mix-heritage girlfriend. It relieved her they hadn't batted an eye.

"Adam is great." Tesha snuck a look at her "boyfriend" who eyed her in return, his expression curious. "He and I have a lot in common."

"That's wonderful," Mrs. Ford smiled broadly. "What do you do?"

They continued to chat for a few minutes, mostly Tesha and Adam's mother, Mr. Ford and Adam watched a television show.

"I was just about to leave, I'll let you have time with Adam." She reached for her purse but his mother stopped her.

"Please stay a minute. I need to make a quick phone call." She looked to Adam's confused father. "Come on Roman, let's give them a minute."

Tesha neared the bed and straightened the sheets for something to do with her hands and searched his face in an attempt to gauge his thought. "I'm going to know how you're doing whether you tell me or your brothers do. It's up to you. And I will come back the day after tomorrow to see you."

His expression was a mixture of hope and shame. "I promise to call you."

"And for the record," Tesha continued. "I won't have you breaking up with me every time we hit a stumbling block. If after a while we decide we're not suited or compatible, then I will accept it." She leaned over him and placed a kiss on his cheek. "I care a lot for you, Adam."

Adam reached up and caressed her face. "I wish things were different. That I was normal." He jutted his chin forward. "I'd rather lose you than ever hurt you."

It was just her luck that the man she'd fallen in love with now wanted nothing to do with her. Tesha lowered until they were eye level. "You need a better reason."

She straightened and turned on her heel and exited the

room. Just outside his parents stood. How much had they overheard? Roman Ford gave her a stiff nod and went inside while his mother lingered.

It was easy to tell Miriam Ford had been a beautiful woman when young because now she remained striking. Where Roman was tall and broad, she was slim and delicate.

She shook her head and rolled her eyes. "Good for you not putting up with that lame excuse from him. Jensen said he's never seen him more taken with a woman." Her eyes softened when she looked to the interior of the room. "I can't begin to understand what my son is going through. But I hope you continue to be patient with him. Of all my sons, Adam is the most loyal, most honorable, of the best temperament. Well, he was before this. And even through this, he rarely lifts his voice, rarely complains."

What the woman said was true. She admired Adam as well as loved him. Tesha wondered what it would be like to see Adam lose his temper. She almost smiled. It would probably be sexy.

Adam's mother hugged her goodbye and Tesha was filled with resolve to fight for her relationship.

She walked through the lobby and once again the same receptionist sat behind the counter. Tesha neared. "Can I send something to be delivered to Adam?"

The woman assured her she could and Tesha left. On the drive back she mused what to do about the current situation with Adam. Sure she could leave well enough alone and move on. After all, she didn't need the complication of a relationship like this. Once she got a good night's sleep, it would be easier to think and ponder what to do.

There was a loud honk and Tesha realized she'd been stopped at a green light lost in thought.

Relationships were so much work.

Chapter Twenty-Six

IT WAS EIGHT in the morning and the house smelled wonderful. A batch of biscuits was ready and Tesha circled around the counter to get them out of the oven. She dashed to open the French doors when Cassie stood out there with a basket full of vegetables. It was Saturday and her friend usually went to the Farmers Market early to pick up fresh produce for the lunch spread.

They made a good team. Tesha would miss Cassie once the whole movie production was over. "Good morning," Cassie shook her head. "I tried to get in through the front door, but you didn't open it when I knocked with my elbow. It hurt. Couldn't knock properly and hold all this crap." She went to the counter and plopped the basket down.

"I'm sorry. I rushed through a shower while the biscuits baked. What about your key?"

Her friend shot her a peeved look. "I couldn't find my key ring, had to grab the spare this morning. I need to get better organized at home. The shop is ship shape, this operation the same. But my poor house suffers. It's a big mess."

Tesha hadn't seen Cassie so flustered before. Decided it was best to let her be. Everyone had one of those days. "Once this is over, how about I come over and help you organize? I'm pretty good at it."

"Would you really do that?" Cassie's eyes shined. "I'm not sure what's wrong with me. I'm so emotional today."

What was wrong with Cassie was that she went to the cupcake shop every day after they finished serving lunch and there was no telling how many hours she put in there. She was burnt out. "Why don't you take today off, Cassie. I'll call Debbie to come over and help out, she's always offering."

"I'll leave as soon as breakfast is over." Cassie sniffed. "I think I need a nap."

Vanessa Morgan and two other actors traipsed down the stairs and straight to the table. Tesha and Cassie went to work pouring coffee and serving breakfast.

An hour later, Tesha walked out to her garden and watered the plants while Kylie ran around in circles barking at the water hose. The puppy yelped when water hit her rump and Tesha let out a chuckle.

Just then the gate flew open and Cassie, who'd gone to Adam's house, ran past her into the house. "I'm leaving now."

Although she'd only caught a glimpse of her friend's face it was enough. Tesha dropped the water hose and rushed in behind her friend. Cassie wiped tears away as she grabbed the basket and her purse. Then let out a soft sob.

"What happened?" Tesha took her by the shoulders. "Why are you crying?"

There was mad crying and there was hurt crying. By the way Cassie was gulping for air, someone had hurt her feelings. She let out a shuddering breath. "It's not important. I'm just so tired otherwise my feelings wouldn't be hurt." She pulled a tissue from her purse and blew her nose with a loud honk. "That man is an arrogant ass."

Tesha looked over her shoulder. There wasn't anyone else in the house. "Which one?"

Shoulders rounded Cassie let her head fall forward. "Jensen Ford said he couldn't imagine anyone making a living baking cupcakes. He then proceeded to say that a cupcake business is the stupidest thing he's ever heard of." She hiccupped and wiped her eyes. "At least I didn't start crying until I got here."

Enough was enough. Tesha guided Cassie to her bedroom and pointed to the bed. "Lay down. Now." With her head down Cassie obediently went to the bed. She dropped her purse on the floor and put the basket next to it. Then she kicked her shoes off and climbed onto the bed, lay her head on the pillow and closed her eyes.

After she drew the curtains over the blinds and turned on a noise machine, Tesha closed the door behind her. She was on a mission and stormed past the two execs who held up coffee cups and looked at her with expectation.

"Serve yourselves," she barked, ignoring their astonished expressions and went through the doors and the garden.

When Jensen saw her coming, he lifted a hand in greeting. "Hey, heard you went to see my brother." He performed a perfect "sexiest man alive" smile. But the closer Tesha got, the more the smile disappeared.

"How could you, Jensen Ford?" Instead of pretending not to hear, the Matt Damon looking cameraman peered around his equipment and watched them with rapt fascination. Another actor rushed into his chair across from Jensen's and looked on, while a man wearing a pink tuxedo top who Tesha figured was a makeup artist or something pretended to arrange an array of brushes and such.

Fist on hips, Tesha stood with her feet apart and ignored the audience. "Because of you, Cassie is at my house crying her eyes out." A bit of a stretch since Cassie was probably sound asleep, but she had cried.

Jensen's eyes widened. "She's crying?"

Tesha neared and pushed her index finger into his chest. "Yes. You hurt her feelings. Just because you are rich and famous doesn't give you the right to insult what she does to make a living. You of all people should understand someone who has the gumption to go after a dream. Cassie is a great person, a hard worker…"

"I didn't mean to insult her. I was mostly joking." He seemed sincere, his eyes looking past her toward the house. Tesha didn't trust him. He was an actor after all.

"You broke her heart and should most definitely apologize to her."

"Definitely." He stood and took a step around her. Tesha stopped him, by yanking on his arm.

"Not now. She had to lie down." Tesha narrowed her eyes at him and leaned forward at the waist. "Just see that you do apologize when you see her and don't ever insult my friend again."

Jensen reared back, his gaze watching her every move. "Jeez, you're the perfect match for Adam. You'll have him under control in no time."

She cocked and eyebrow and he held his hands up. "I'll apologize to Cassie next time I see her."

"Oh, you better." She spun on her heel and walked away almost mowing over a gawker who jumped out of her way.

THE AFTERNOON WAS pleasant enough. Mrs. Miller and her duo served lunch and Cassie had awakened refreshed after two hours and left to go work at the shop.

Mrs. Miller gave the counter one last swipe with her wet cloth. "I'm going to Nashville to visit Adam," she announced. "But first I best stop at the store and make sure Jerry hasn't blown anything up." She shook her head in annoyance. "He's a hard worker, but a bit too excited about the power tools."

"Can you take something to Adam for me?" Tesha went to the cabinets and began to pull things out. "I'll whip up a quick half recipe of my biscuits for him."

"Good idea." Mrs. Miller poured a cup of coffee and settled into a chair. "If that doesn't make him better, nothing will. You should market those, they are amazing."

Tesha began measuring and mixing. "What brought on this sudden impulse to visit him?"

"I have to make sure he's here for the Fourth of July celebration. He promised he would, but I better make sure he doesn't back out."

With all the commotion of the movie production Tesha had forgotten about the celebration. The town was planning a surprise during the celebration for Adam. "Have you given any thought to the fact that fireworks may be a bad idea for someone with PTSD?"

Mrs. Miller nodded. "We only need him to be present for the mayor's speech. It's in the afternoon, so plenty of time for him to be safe and sound in his house before the fireworks begin. Of course that doesn't account for Arnold Moore across the way who puts on a fireworks display of his own during his annual Patriotic party."

"I wonder how he dealt with it the past years?" Tesha mused aloud.

"Who knows," Mrs. Miller replied. "Maybe headphones and loud music."

Tesha cut out the biscuits and placed them onto a flat cookie sheet. "Please tell him I say hello and am planning to visit him. I hope to have a chance but it looks dismal with all this extra work lately. I'm looking forward to him seeing him later this week."

Mrs. Miller gave her a strange look. "You don't look ecstatic about it at all."

"That because he plans to break up with me." Tesha blew her bangs out of her eyes. "He's being a butt head."

"Men tend to become idiots when scared or embarrassed," Mrs. Miller told her and looked out the window. "Well, look at that. Is that Vanessa Morgan with her tongue down Matt Damon's throat?"

"It's the cameraman, not Matt Damon." Tesha insisted while looking out toward the couple.

"I don't think she'd kiss a cameraman like that," Mrs. Miller replied while craning her neck to get a better view.

Chapter Twenty-Seven

ADAM ASSESSED THE utilitarian hospital room. Grey walls, two fake oil paintings of outdoor scenes, one window with shades, no curtains, a chest of drawers against the wall with his personal belongings atop, a nightstand with a digital clock and a lamp with a crooked shade. That one was his doing.

If one weren't depressed before coming here, the damn room would sure do it. He swung his legs to the floor and went to the bathroom. At least he wasn't restrained anymore and could pee on his own.

Things had gotten bad during his last flashback. He'd lost control, wanted to hurt someone, kill himself. After weeks without a flashback, this one had struck him hard. Maybe not so much that it was worse, but that he'd not expected it. Had begun to hope they wouldn't return. So much anger infused with fury had turned into a mass of tears, screams and pain.

He washed his hands and looked at his wrists. They were still scratched and bruised from fighting the restraints. In the mirror he studied his face. His bottom lip was healing, the bruises on the side of his jaw fading. One of his brothers. Caden. He'd attacked Caden when he'd attempted to subdue him.

God what if he'd hurt his mom or dad even? Although

Roman Ford was a big guy, that didn't mean he could handle a man full of rage, blind with fear.

There was a tentative knock, Adam walked out of the bathroom to find Mrs. Miller standing in the doorway holding a basket. The familiar scent of Tesha's ham and cheese biscuits made his mouth water.

"Well, you look good as new," Mrs. Miller exclaimed and bustled past him to place the small basket on the bedside table. She turned and smiled at him. "Came to break you out."

Adam chuckled and brought a chair from across the room for her to sit. "I could use help breaking out. They keep this place pretty well monitored. What do you have in mind?"

It was good to see the older woman who'd always made him feel at ease. Even during his darkest moods when he'd first started renovating Vince's house, she'd never made him feel ill at ease. Her easy nature and understanding gazes never wavered.

"Go on, eat up." She lifted a small plate from the basket and placed two biscuits on it. "She sent six. So you have plenty for later." A small squeeze bottle of honey was produced and Mrs. Miller handed it to him. "Tesha said you liked to pour honey over them. I thought it was a grand idea and that's how I eat mine now."

While Adam ate, Mrs. Miller told him all about the Fourth of July celebration plans. She filled him in on the goings on at the movie production to include her sighting of who she thought was Matt Damon pretending to be a cameraman.

"Tesha says she can't wait for you to come back to your house," Mrs. Miller told him and raised her eyebrows. "She also told me you plan to break things off."

"And you're going to try and talk me out of it?"

"Goodness, no." Mrs. Miller gave him a stern look taking in his surprised expression. "You're not good enough for her, dear. She deserves a man who loves her enough to fight for her. I think that pilot boy was nice enough. Maybe she'll date him again."

At the mention of Malloy, Adam stiffened. "Has he been back?"

"Not that I know of," Mrs. Miller produced a can of energy drink from her purse and popped it open. "But he is a looker." She winked at Adam and took a long drink.

"Should you be drinking those?" Adam eyed the can. "They have a lot of caffeine."

"Who knows?" A tingle of laughter and Mrs. Miller took another swallow. "That may be why I'm addicted to them."

Had Tesha mentioned Malloy to Mrs. Miller because she was already planning to date him? If that jerk was sniffing around Tesha, he would pound him into the ground. "Why do you think Malloy is a better choice for Tesha?"

"I don't know that I would say a better choice. If I had my say I'd pick you as the perfect man for her. You both have a lot of healing to do and it takes someone who is broken to understand what the other is going through. She is patient and willing to give you space and Tesha has spunk. She confronted Jensen Ford in front of the entire film crew when he hurt Cassie's feelings. She is not one to take any stuff."

Adam looked at his empty plate then to the basket. He took another biscuit from the zip lock bag and resealed it. "I miss these."

"So, will I see you on the fourth?"

ADAM LET HIMSELF into the house. It was quiet, seemed all the film crew was out behind the house shooting in the woods. He wondered what the 'super-hero' was up to. His bedroom was in pretty good shape even through Jensen's things were strewn about. He lowered the cardboard box he'd carried in and began to collect anything that wasn't his and then took the filled box out to the hallway. Once he emptied the room of Jensen's belongings, he took them across the hall to a spare bedroom and placed everything on the bed. It looked to be empty. Maybe whoever had been using it was done. Next Adam went back to his bedroom and stripped the bed.

"What are you doing?" It was the bossy woman who always carried a clipboard in her hand and a chip on her shoulder.

"Laundry," Adam replied pouring detergent in to the machine and hitting the 'start' button. "I'm washing my bedding and I'm moving back into my bedroom. My brother is now staying across the hall." He pointed at her clipboard. "Make a note on there that I will punch him in the face if he tries to move back into my bedroom."

The woman took a step back and blinked. "Maurice Black is supposed to use that room." She frowned down at her clipboard. "It won't do, you have to move out."

Adam neared the woman and didn't stop until well inside her personal space. "No."

"I'll speak to Mr. Bernstein about this. He won't be happy." She clip-clopped away and out the front door. Adam went to the kitchen and stopped. Everything was different. Where the hell was his coffee maker?

He was just putting off the inevitable. It was time to face Tesha, to make a decision about what was best. For the last couple of days while waiting to be discharged, he'd changed his mind many times.

Was it selfish of him to remain with her just because he hated the idea of her belonging to anyone else? What if he hurt her one day? What if the whole relationship thing was something he couldn't handle?

It was all so foreign. The idea of being accountable to someone and caring for another person scared the shit out of him.

An older man with a receding hairline, wire framed glasses and an expensive watch came in. He searched the space until finding Adam. It must be Mr. Bernstein who the clipboard lady had threatened him with.

"Ah, there you are. Come along. It's time." He waved for Adam to follow him.

Out of morbid curiosity, he did.

Half an hour later Jensen hovered over Adam who lay on the ground arms and legs in all directions. "I can't breathe," Adam told his brother. "What the hell was that?"

"It's a cross between a dragon and a man. Pretty neat, huh? Well, that's not what you saw, but that's what it will be on the screen. They hit you with a huge padded block of wood."

Adam rolled to his hands and knees. "I thought I was supposed to land on an air mattress or something."

"Nah, it's more realistic if you land on the ground. Dude you bounced." Jensen sank onto the grass next to him laughing. "You screamed like a girl, too."

"It fucking hurt." Adam tried to punch Jensen, but it pained him to move. "What if I broke a rib?"

Jensen stopped laughing and began to poke at him while Adam batted his hands away. "You're not a doctor, don't touch me."

"You're fine." Jensen stood and held his hand down to help Adam to his feet. "That was fun, huh? Wanna see it?"

A wide grin broke on Adam's face. "Yeah." The brothers jogged to the playback monitors.

Chapter Twenty-Eight

"Adam is over there," Cassie announced when she entered after delivering cupcakes to the dining area behind the house. "He and that jackass were running around doing something with the film crew from what I could see."

Tesha's stomach tumbled at the mention of Adam's name. "Jensen hasn't spoken to you yet?"

"He tried, but I told him I didn't want to hear anything he had to say." Cassie huffed and put her hands on her hips. "I don't like him."

It would be wrong to point out that Cassie happened to mention Jensen several times a day so Tesha shrugged. "Yes, he is a bit arrogant. But I suppose fame does that to people."

She wondered how long it would be before Adam made an appearance to tell her he'd not changed his mind and wanted to break things off. It would not surprise her if he didn't come over at all and just stand by what he'd said at the clinic. Whatever happened, she'd prepared herself for it. Either way she was moving forward, whether as a single girl or as Adam Ford's girlfriend, her plan to make *The Haven* a place for healing and rest would continue. Enough with the entire crazy next-door neighbor crush thing.

Cassie left not much later and from what the actors had said that morning at breakfast, filming would run late so that gave her a free afternoon and evening to herself. Tesha took advantage of the few hours of solitude. She took a book and a glass of sweet tea and settled into one of the wicker chairs outside. Kylie ran around in the garden for a few minutes and then jumped on the seat next to her and promptly fell asleep.

The words on the page blurred as sleepiness threatened to take over. Tesha yawned and looked up to see Adam opening the gate. She took a fortifying breath. "Hello."

Adam neared and looked down at her. "You were about to fall asleep weren't you?"

Tesha stretched her legs across the seat of the chair and curved them around Kylie, not leaving any room for Adam to join them. "Uh huh."

"Thank you for the biscuits." His eyes scanned over her and instantly every inch of skin came to attention.

What was it about love that made one so sensitive? Every single one of his movements, expressions, and mannerisms affected her. Tesha nodded. "I know you like them. It's what girlfriends do." Okay that was a bit of a dig, but she couldn't take it back now.

Adam remained solemn, as usual a master of keeping his thoughts hidden.

It was not in her nature to play games and Tesha definitely did not want to extend the inevitable. If anything the sooner they ended things, the faster she could get the crying, heart break over with. She stood and faced him. "Come inside, please." If they were going to break up, she preferred it to be in private. Whether he dumped her or the other way around, hopefully there wouldn't be any witnesses.

Once inside, Adam seemed to relax. He followed her to her

office. It was the only room beside her bedroom where they would not be disturbed. Tesha stopped and waited for him to talk. Based on his first words she'd gauge what he intended and act accordingly. Her plan was formulated and practiced.

He didn't speak a word. Instead moved around the room stopping occasionally and glancing at her. Sometimes his gaze was searching, other times he looked almost as if he wanted to devour her.

Enough was enough. She gripped her hands together in front of her. "Adam, it shouldn't be so hard to tell me what you came to say. Let's just end things. If you are not ready for a relationship, then it's probably for the best. I'm sorry things didn't work out."

He listened to her and then looked down to the floor. When he neared, she stood frozen, waiting for the goodbye kiss or hug or whatever he was going to do. Already tears were threatening and she blinked doing her best to not let him see how the situation affected her.

His hands were firm on her upper arms as he held her and looked into her eyes. "I love you."

"What?" Why was he saying this now?

His irises darkened until almost midnight blue. "I'm in love with you. I don't want to lose you."

"Oh." She wasn't sure what to say and thankfully it didn't matter because his mouth covered hers and his arms surrounded her pulling her against his chest. He deepened the kiss and she wasn't sure whether to pull him closer or shove him away. They needed to talk.

His hands slid down her back while his mouth traveled from the corner of her mouth to her neck. Tesha moaned. She loved his hungry kisses, his touches full of want.

Although her brain told her they needed to stop and discuss things, her body had other ideas. Her body won, Tesha managed to find one of Adam's hands. She pulled him to her bedroom.

Half an hour later, they lay panting next to each other on her bed. Her blouse and bra were shoved above her breasts and her skirt looked more like a belt; it was most uncomfortable now that her sanity returned. Adam seemed to be just as uncomfortable, his pants and briefs pushed below his butt.

"We—we should talk," Tesha managed to say while fighting to breathe.

"Now?" Adam rolled to his side, lifted to his elbow and peered down at her.

"Yes, now. Adam, we need to clear things up. I have to know where I stand. I can't keep allowing my damn hormones to take over," Tesha muttered yanking her clothing back into place.

"Don't you think you should readjust your clothes?" He had to do something and fast before she lost control again and attacked him. It was hard to keep her gaze from his exposed parts.

"You're not going to break up with me are you?" Finally he began to pull his pants up. "I thought you said you were going to fight me on it."

Tesha slid to the edge of the bed and sat. God how could she keep contradicting herself? One minute she told him it was over and the next she was in bed with him. They were both constantly confused and saying one thing and doing the opposite of what they should be doing.

"If you are not going to fight alongside me, then it won't work. One person can't do it alone for a relationship to work." It was time she set things straight, put it on the line. Time to buck up.

If he didn't like what she said, he could walk out because he wasn't the man she thought he was.

Tesha turned to him and held his face in her palms looking into his eyes. "I believe in you, Adam. You are strong, intelligent, and resilient. You didn't survive the war just to come home and give up. You made it because in spite of everything, all you saw and lost, you have a purpose. It's time for you to fulfill it. Every set back is just that, a stumbling block. If anything, you should know those are to be kicked in the ass. If we are going to be in this together, I need to know that no matter what, you will keep trying. I lost David to that damn war. I don't want to lose another man I love just as much to it. Don't give that damn situation any more power over you. Over us."

He kissed her, not a passionate kiss, but a sweet kiss. It was nice to see his face soften and the corners of his lips curve up for an instant. He was such a somber man usually.

"Tell me what you're thinking," Tesha asked.

Adam cleared his throat. "When I was an officer, I was a good one. It was up to me to be the soldier responsible for keeping my unit together during the worst of times. I managed to keep myself on task while everything around us was going to hell."

He shifted and looked at his hands. "You know, I always kept a steady eye out for my men. I knew when one was about to lose it, when they were too weak mentally for certain missions. I could tell when their heads were not in it. In those instances, I had to talk them up, to get them to the place they needed to be in order to survive. It never occurred to me that one day, I would be the one that needed help."

"I love you, Adam. Tell me you'll fight for us." Tesha waited, her heart pounding as she recognized uncertainty in his expression. His eyes downcast Adam exhaled.

"I will do my best."

"Not good enough."

He straightened and looked into her eyes. This time he did smile, the corners of his eyes crinkling. "Yes, ma'am. I will fight and we will win. With you by my side, I can't see how I can lose."

"That's my man." Tesha let out a yelp when he tackled her back to the mattress and covered her body with his.

He was so breathtakingly handsome. His playful side melted her heart.

While he held her arms over her head, Adam nipped at her lips. "I'm spending the night here and tonight we'll make love properly." He kissed her, his lips demanding and hot. Her body instantly reacted.

"I can't wait."

"Tell me again."

"What?" Tesha smiled at him.

"That you love me."

"I love you."

"Good."

That evening Tesha took care to ensure everything was perfect. Although excited at the prospect of spending the evening with Adam, she was also cautiously optimistic about how well things would go once they settled into a relationship. There were many things to learn about him, many questions about his life and his expectations of her.

Of course that was the way with every couple. Tesha reminded herself. Little by little they would discover each other and tonight was the first of many evenings they'd share.

The candles flickered casting romantic shadows over the table as they ate beef tips in wine sauce and nibbled on young green beans from the Farmers Market. Neither ate a lot. For some reason Tesha was nervous and excited at the same time in knowing they'd end the evening by making love. The few times they'd had sex it was not planned, but spontaneous. This was different. She wondered if Adam was nervous as well.

Tesha drank from her glass of wine. "Mrs. Miller said you promised to be at the Fourth of July celebration."

Adam nodded. "Yep, I will be there. I may even wear something nice, like a suit." His lips curved. "Maybe you'll find me irresistible in a suit."

Her belly did a quick allie-oop. "I find you irresistible in most anything."

His eyes darkened. "The feeling is mutual." He stood and pushed his chair back. "As good as dinner was, I can't wait to taste dessert."

"Its cupcakes," Tesha said her voice fading when his meaning became clear as his gaze raked down her body. She was dessert.

The only light in the bedroom came from the kitchen. The shadowy room was set perfectly for lovers. The bed with its off-white linens topped by a fluffed up comforter, invited them to lie upon it.

Tesha allowed Adam to undress her. His lips pressed to her shoulder as he slipped her spaghetti strap down and then did the same to the other side. The first button was followed by the next and then he licked his way across the tops of her breasts. The combination of the actions and his hot breath was more erotic than any daydream she'd had.

"Take your dress off." The command was soft, yet strong. Adam took a step away from her and watched.

Her fingers trembled as she released the final two buttons. The dress slipped to her hips leaving her exposed, nude from the waist up. She shimmied out of it and let it puddle at her feet. In nothing but her thong and strappy sandals, she stepped free of the clothes.

When she bent to remove the shoes, Adam stopped her. "No, don't. Lie on the bed and watch me."

That was an order she was definitely in favor of. Her eyes devoured the tall beautiful man who pulled his t-shirt over his head exposing his well-formed chest. He locked gazes with her and then looked down to his jeans. Without words he guided her to where he wanted her to look. His hands were steady as he unzipped his pants and pulled them down, briefs and all. He stood proud, his thick erection jutting up toward his flat stomach.

"I'm yours, Tesha. Will always be."

For the first time since meeting him, Tesha realized how much it cost Adam to open himself. To trust another human to be there for him, to not abandon him. And she would do her best to be that person.

Tesha lifted her hand and beckoned him. "Come to bed. Show me with that delicious body how much you are mine."

Their bodies collided with an intensity that made her shudder. Adam's hands held her face and his mouth took hers. She reached around his waist and slid her hands down his taut bottom cupping the firmness and pulled him closer, rubbing herself against his hardness.

He made some guttural happy sounds and Tesha nibbled at his neck and shoulder while sliding her hand down to his upper thighs and caressing his muscles.

Adam rolled them over and pulled her to straddle him. Without needing encouragement, she wrapped her fingers around his penis and slid her hand up and down. He closed his eyes and threw his head back onto the pillow. He trusted her. Although his eyes opened when she lifted to guide him to enter her and watched for those few seconds. When he closed his eyes again, she knew he'd let his guard down and allowed her free access to him.

Tesha lowered slowly to let her body adjust to his girth. Both let out a soft moan at being fully joined. She rested her palms on his chest and began to rock her hips, sliding him in an out in a steady motion.

Adam's hands covered her breasts. His thumbs toyed with her nipples. She let her head fall back at the many wonderful sensations filling her. When she began to lose control, Adam took her hips and held her still. "Not yet."

He lifted her gently and off of him. "Get on your hands and knees, Tesha."

The way he took control was so erotic she almost came at the husky words. She complied and he guided her to the edge of the bed. Adam stood behind her, lifted her bottom and drove back into her. She looked over her shoulder and met his heated gaze. His eyes flickered to her bottom. "You have an amazing ass."

Before she could answer, he thrust fully into her and she cried out. "Oh God!"

From slow and steady to hard and pounding, Adam moved according to what her body demanded from him. Tesha was on the verge of losing control. "Harder, please!" she cried out. "I'm so close."

Without losing his rhythm, Adam held her hips with one hand and reached around her with the other and flicked her clitoris. She shuddered and burst into pieces, her face digging into the bedding.

Although lost in the abyss of passionate haze, Tesha felt Adam shudder then cry out while he drove into her a few more times then shuddered. He withdrew after a few moments and pulled her onto the bed. Their bodies were slick with sweat, they lay legs and arms entangled.

THERE WAS NOTHING better than waking up with her lover. Tesha snuggled into Adams hard body, her head on his shoulder, the next morning. She draped her arm around his waist and listened to the steady heartbeat.

He slept soundly. She wasn't sure what time they'd finally fallen asleep. Her lips curved at picturing how they'd lay entwined around each other fighting sleep and talking about everything and nothing. He'd shared his thoughts about the upcoming celebration and had even made her laugh when telling her about his walk-on part in the movie where he died within seconds. Attacked by a dragon man monster of some sort.

She kissed his chest and slipped from the bed. It was time to start breakfast. As tempting as it was to remain in bed with her handsome boyfriend, her duties called. Besides Cassie would arrive any minute.

A few minutes later, showered and dressed, she glanced once more at the slumbering man and after a deep sigh headed to the kitchen.

Chapter Twenty-Nine

"When do the folks get here?" Jensen grumbled and played with the home fries on his plate.

Adam and his brother had gone into town to have lunch because Jensen insisted he was sick of being on-site for so many days in a row. Now at the town's small diner, Adam wondered why his brother remained in a sour mood.

"Mom said they'd be here early tomorrow morning. They are excited about the cookout with Liam Neeson. It was cool of you to set it up."

Jensen shrugged, picked up a fry and studied it. "The fries are good here." He dunked it into a puddle of ketchup and ate it. Then stared out the window.

Adam let out a breath. "What's bugging you?"

His brother's hazel eyes flickered to him and then back out the window. "I was told by a certain someone I'm a sucky actor."

"Are you?"

Jensen's eyes rounded and his eyebrows rose. "No. I happen to think I'm pretty fuckin' good."

"Then who cares what someone says." Adam plucked a fry from his brother's plate and ate it.

"Hey, get your own."

"I already ate all mine."

Jensen moved his plate closer. "What do you think?"

"I think you're selfish," Adam eyed the fries. "And I think you're a great actor. Everyone is entitled to think whatever he or she wants. Jensen, you know that. Not everyone's going to like you."

"I know." This was a side of his brother seldom seen. Jensen was the cocky self-assured guy who rarely let anything get to him. Something else was up.

"Why did they say it? Who said you're a bad actor?"

"The cupcake chick."

"Cassie Tucker? She's really sweet. I don't see her saying something like that. Could it be that you called her 'cupcake chick' to her face?"

Jensen let out a breath. "I was in the middle of apologizing for saying I didn't feel someone could be serious about making a living baking cupcakes when she said, 'I think you are a terrible actor and don't know how you manage to be successful.'" He frowned down at his plate and pushed it to Adam. "I'm not selfish."

"No, you're not. You give Caden cars and you offered to buy the folks a new house. You've always given to charity and don't skimp when it comes to gifts for any of us. But you have to admit, things have come easy for you, dude. And it was not cool to say those things to Cassie."

"I had to fight to get the acting roles just like everyone else." Jensen became defensive, his nostrils flared and lips formed in a straight line. "I work hard."

Adam held his hands up. "Yes, I agree you work hard. But it took you a portion of the time it takes most people to make it. That pretty face opens doors for you. Shit, you even told me your very first role was a coveted one. Everyone loves you. I think Lady Luck takes care of you."

"Cassie Tucker obviously doesn't love me."

It was hard not to laugh at the almost pout. "She's probably angry because you insulted her livelihood, whether on purpose or not."

Adam wondered why it mattered so much to Jensen. Could it be his rich and famous brother had finally met the one woman who didn't fall at his feet?

The waitress came up and refilled their glasses with fresh Coke. She smiled timidly at Jensen. "Can I get a picture with you before you leave? My husband and kids will be excited to see it."

It was interesting to watch Jensen transform into his public persona. He gifted the waitress with his famous wide smile. "Of course, it would be my pleasure."

After Jensen took several pictures with the waitress and others at the restaurant and leaving a fifty-dollar tip, they left.

Jensen assessed him and cocked an eyebrow. "It's nice to see you so relaxed. So…normal. Things must be good with Tesha."

A smile curved Adam's lips. "Yeah, things are great."

His brother came closer and they did a one-arm hug. "Good."

They stood next to Jensen's bike. He straddled his motorcycle and put his helmet on. "I'm going for a long ride. See ya later."

Adam watched his brother ride off. Their mother hated the motorcycle, but Jensen was a good rider. It was one of the things he did to find time alone. On a bike, he was away from the lights, cameras, and cell phones. And right now, Jensen needed to get away from Cassie Tucker too.

Adam looked down the center of the town toward where he lived. Smalltown, USA, this was what he'd fought for overseas, what his friend died for. And what David Washington, Tesha's husband had given up his life and wife for.

The red, white, and blue banners hung from street lights, bunting was fastened to the awnings of the small town's storefronts and men worked on assembling a stage of sorts in front of the library.

Interesting that he didn't feel like the hero everyone insisted he was. A survivor, yes, but a man who wanted a normal life was more who he was.

THAT WEEKEND, THE entire town crowded the streets. Adam stood beside the mayor, holding Tesha's hand. She flexed her fingers and he realized he was squeezing it for dear life. "It's okay. You'll do great," she whispered in his ear.

Across from the small elevated stage where they stood, he could see most of the production team was there as well as Jensen, Vanessa Morgan, his parents, and brother Caden. Tristan could not get away from work.

The small high school band played an off tune rendition of the Army song followed by a singer who strummed a guitar and sang admirably well *Proud to be an American*. The mayor asked for silence and he spoke into the microphone.

"It's not every day one meets a hero. It's not common for one to walk amongst us on a daily basis. Fortunately, one came home here to Lovely, for which we are thankful. Each man and woman who's served this country is a hero in their own right. But there are heroes and then there are men like Adam Ford. A man who not only put his life on the line for his country but went the extra mile and faced certain death to save the lives of four of his men. Today it is our honor to acknowledge this American hero with a small token of this town's appreciation."

The mayor waved his arm and a banner was removed from the side of the library. "We have named our new library the Adam Mark Ford Library." The tall thin man then looked to Adam. "And this is also for you, it will be mounted on the wall in the foyer." He motioned for a covering to be removed from a large framed painting on an easel. It depicted a helicopter which he piloted. The three men who he'd saved that day in Afghanistan stood on the ground saluting. One man, who he assumed was supposed to be Vinnie, was inside the helicopter. Adam's throat closed and he felt his legs threaten to give out.

Tesha leaned against him and sniffed. "What a beautiful painting. You are such a brave man, Adam."

Her words sunk in and gave him the strength to step up to the podium and speak the few words he'd memorized. He thanked the mayor and the town for the honor. Past the crowd he looked to the sky and swore he felt Vince smiling at him. His breathing hitched, but thankfully, Tesha took his hand again and immediately he relaxed. "I am honored and thank you. The real heroes were those who gave their lives for this country. I am proud to have served alongside them."

"I WOULDN'T GO in there." That evening his father was outside in Tesha's garden with a putter and a bucket of balls. "The women are plotting something."

Adam peered through the glass. His mother, Tesha, and Cassie sat around a table with glasses of wine. Mrs. Miller stood by the counter and waved her arms while talking. The women erupted into peals of laughter.

"Yep, looks pretty scary." He eyed his dad and pointed to the larger area outside the garden. "You want to practice out there where you can actually hit the ball farther?"

Roman Ford shook his head. "Nope, I'm supposed to corral you, Caden, and Jensen. I think we're going to have dinner in a few. If they're going to be drunk and disorderly, I don't think we should join them until we have to."

Adam looked to the sky; the sun would be setting in an hour. It was obvious what they planned. To get him inside where he'd not be exposed to the sounds of fireworks. Unfortunately he'd just seen the movie crew with a golf cart full of all kinds of sparklers and other things. They planned a full on display in his backyard.

"Dad. I think I need to leave for a few hours. If I drive west for about an hour, there is nothing out there but open road. I'll camp out overnight, it should be quiet."

"I'll go with you." Tesha stood at the doorway. Her face was flushed and her eyes bright.

"How many glasses of wine have you had?"

"Two," she said and held up three fingers. She looked at her fingers and began to giggle. "Okay maybe I had three."

His mother walked out and looked at her husband. "Where are Jensen and Caden?"

Half an hour later, they all huddled around the table and ate a huge pot-roast Cassie and Tesha had cooked. Adam seemed to be the only one with an appetite. He ate seconds and eyed Tesha's plate contemplating finishing hers. Jensen and Cassie avoided looking at each other. Caden eyed Adam with suspicion and Mrs. Miller kept refilling everyone's drinks.

Boom! The loud sound made everyone jump. Tesha hiccupped, her rounded eyes on him.

Jensen growled and stood. "I'll tell 'em to stop immediately."

Adam stood. Everyone watched him with varying expressions that ranged from fearful, Cassie, to cautious, his mother. He met Tesha's gaze and held out his hand to her. "Let's go outside and watch."

Unlike everyone else, Tesha jumped up and clapped her hands. "Yes, let's." She gripped his hand and smiled up at him.

They trouped outside and before long were settled into either blankets on the ground or lawn chairs. Jensen brought some beers for the men and the women held refilled wine glasses.

Fireworks burst in the sky, different shimmering colors crisscrossing the darkness. With his woman settled between his legs, Adam leaned back on his arms enjoying Tesha's soft curves.

She looked up at him. "Are you okay?"

Adam frowned. "Not really."

"Do you want to go inside?"

He wagged his eyebrows. "I need to hide under the blanket with you."

The sound of Tesha's laughter made his mother look over and she beamed at them. Lights burst overhead a myriad of colorful sparks rained down and his heart burst with pride. He loved this country and the one thing this holiday was about. His country.

This was what home felt like, fireworks overhead, his family surrounding him, and his woman in his arms.

Finally, he understood what Vince meant by living a life that was enough for his too.

He'd do his best to honor his friend by making it a great life. With Tesha beside him, he couldn't fail.

"I love you," he whispered into Tesha's ear.

Tesha looked up at him and he kissed her lightly. "I know," she replied.

Chapter Thirty

"YOU HAVE NOT stopped grinning since you walked in." Cassie eyed Tesha while frosting cupcakes.

It was early afternoon and they were at Cassie's cupcake shop, Tesha at her usual corner table drinking coffee and toying with an espresso cupcake Cassie asked her to test.

It was good, but not as good as her favorite caramel one. "I'm so happy I'm terrified," Tesha admitted. "Is it strange to feel as if it's too good to be true?"

Cassie shook her head. "I don't think so. Especially after all you've been through."

In a few weeks, the movie production in Lovely would be done and other than a couple of short one or two day returns in the next few months, everything would return to its normal quiet pace. Tesha couldn't wait to find out what it entailed for her and Adam. He would go back to Nashville during the week to work and come home for the weekends.

She wasn't overly happy with that arrangement, and already they planned for her to come and stay in his corporate apartment in Nashville the following week.

Cassie leaned on the high table and rested her chin on her hands. "It's all so romantic. The way you two look at each other, my goodness you can set things on fire with all those sparks."

They laughed and Tesha couldn't help but grin. "I know, he's so yummy isn't he?"

"He is," Cassie agreed. "Too bad his brother is a big butthead."

"I don't think Jensen is so bad. He's a bit of a character, but it may be he's spoiled." Tesha laughed at Cassie's eye roll. "You know what I think? I think you find him attractive and it bugs you."

"Oh, look, here comes Mrs. Miller." Cassie hurried to the door with too much enthusiasm.

Mrs. Miller bustled in and looked from Cassie to Tesha. "Oh, I didn't think I'd find you two here. Cassie don't you take a day off, goodness sakes, it's Sunday." She turned to Tesha. "What about you, I figured you'd be spending the day with Adam."

"He went to Nashville, he has an early appointment with Dr. Mitchell in the morning." Tesha pointed to Cassie. "She has no excuse for being here, other than she's avoiding Jensen Ford."

"I am not." Cassie started the mixer and turned her back to them.

Mrs. Miller shrugged and sat down with Tesha. "I was out for my afternoon walk and saw the lights on in here." She tapped her fingers on the tabletop. "Have you seen Matt Damon?"

"It's not him," Tesha told her, unable to stop the giggle. "It's a cameraman who looks a lot like him, but I assure you Matt Damon is not here, Mrs. Miller. And no, I have not seen him. They are not around today. Most of them went to Nashville yesterday as soon as filming was done for the week."

"Hmpf." Mrs. Miller stood. "Cassie girl, give me three cupcakes, any flavor. Surprise me. I'm off, need to get home and straighten up. With my trip up north and all this catering business, I have a lot of housework to do and I need fuel."

TESHA LOVED THE view from Adam's corporate apartment. It overlooked Nashville, all the lights and contagious excitement seemed to float in the air. They'd dined in a beautiful posh restaurant and now she held a glass of wine and waited for him to come from the bedroom. He'd said to wait a minute. She assumed he was in the bathroom and took advantage to explore the spacious home.

It was elegant, but sterile. The only personal affect in the living room was a picture of Adam and his brothers on the fireplace mantle. The couches were black leather. On both sides, matching clean cut pecan sleek tables and lamps.

Just as she put the glass down Adam walked out and she lost her breath. He'd removed his black suit jacket and loosened the tie. His hair just to the top of his collar was styled and perfectly in place. Above his eyes, his brows were hard slashes and his sensuous lips curved in a soft smile. "You look beautiful with the lights behind you." He came closer and kissed her.

"You are amazingly handsome. I love looking at you." Tesha allowed him to pull her into an embrace.

They walked onto the balcony and looked down at the city. "It's a perfect night," Tesha told him. "I have been to Nashville before, but it's so much better from up here."

Adam kissed her temple. "I agree. I love this town."

She took a fortifying breath. "Adam, do you plan to move back here? You can't work in Nashville and live in Lovely. It will be too much."

"I've been thinking about it." He frowned. "I can work four days a week and spend three days in Lovely. I'm sure it will work since Tristan plans to remain CEO and I'm a partner, but keeping more of a secondary role."

"Were you the CEO before?"

He nodded. "Yes, I took over Ford Enterprises after my father retired."

"Then why did you leave and go into the Army?"

He looked to the lights for a while before answering. "I was a young CEO, too young really. My business partner, Alex Grey, had gone to New York on business. Terribly timing, he died in the Twin Towers attack. Time passed and I couldn't stand not doing anything about it. When Caden decided to join the Army, I wanted to go with him, protect him. He lied and had joined the Air Force 'cause he figured one of us would follow him." He smiled and shook his head.

"Anyway, once I convinced Tristan to take over for me, I joined up and went over. Probably a dumb thing, it's not like it brought Alex back and there wasn't any way for me to protect Caden."

Tesha leaned against him and took his hand. "Several men are alive because you chose to go. Everything happens for a reason."

"Yes, I spent six years in the military, almost all of it over there." He shrugged. "But it's behind me now. From now on, you're my life."

It was good to hear he could speak of such things and not drop the walls and shut her out. Instead he remained relaxed although a bit restless. He flexed the fingers of the hand she wasn't holding.

"Are you all right, Adam?"

He pressed his lips together and then blew out. "I'm a bit nervous."

"Maybe we should sit. I can give you a back rub."

His eyebrows rose. "Would you?"

She chuckled. Men were so easy sometimes. "Of course."

He didn't move, the worrisome wariness became apparent and Tesha braced herself. Something was amiss. She'd tried to ignore it all day, but the way he kept studying her when thinking she didn't notice was something new. As if he assessed something. It had put her on edge.

"Tesha," Adam started and then swallowed. "There are times when I'm still not sure it's possible for me to have a normal life."

Where was this going? She took a step back and held on to the bannister. "You have to give yourself time, Adam. I understand if you need space. If at any time, you want me to give you time alone, just let me know. It won't be easy, but I will do it. I'll stay in Lovely and not see you. But I won't give up on us."

"I don't want that." He looked away toward the city scene as if the answer to whatever bothered him were out there. "Damn it, Tesha, I am so fucking confused."

"What about, Adam?" She took his hands and pulled him inside. "Let's sit down. Tell me what you're thinking."

He didn't sit. Instead he paced from one end of the room

to the other and then stopped and looked at her. Fear and anxiety mixed in the depths of his eyes. "We've been through so much. You and I have lost a part of ourselves to that damn war. I am never going to be a whole man. I know you will always miss David. Sometimes I hate it all so much."

"I know." Tesha blinked to keep tears at bay. "How I wish there was a way to take your pain. The flashbacks that torment you."

Adam closed his eyes and took a shaky breath. "Because of you, I am a better man. Deep down I know it will be a long road. It's not fair to put the burden on you." His hand shook when he raked his fingers through is hair. "Do you think it's possible for us to have a good life together? Because I can't imagine it without you."

Her heart skipped and Tesha stood. She didn't go to him, instead managed a watery smile.

"No, Adam. You and I will never have a good life together. We will have a great life. Because we," she motioned back and forth between them, "we appreciate each day. The one good thing to come from the crap life dealt us is that we know things can always be worse. So we appreciate each good moment more."

Adam walked to her and pulled Tesha into his arms. She leaned against his chest and wrapped her arms around his waist. His voice was husky with emotion. "You're right. How did I get so lucky to find you?"

The sound of his heart thumping steadily against her ear was reassuring and Tesha closed her eyes marveling at how much she loved him. "God Adam, you are my new life. I love you so much."

"I have something important to ask you." Adam took her chin and lifted her face to him. Her heart skipped. What more could he want to say?

"I have been second guessing all day whether or not I could convince you to share your life with me. I want you to be my wife. Be my partner for the rest of my life." Adam lowered on one knee and held up a ring. "Will you please marry me?"

Her mouth fell open and then she grinned down at him.

"Tesha, will you marry me and move to Nashville."

Tesha nodded and let out a shaky breath. "Yes. Oh my God, yes!"

He slipped the ring onto her finger and stood, pulling her to him and kissing her until she was dizzy with want. He lifted his face and smiled down at her. "Now, how about that back rub?"

Her mind began to spin. "I'll move to Nashville, once we get married. I want to finish up my job with the movie production and then decide about the house." Tesha bit her lip. "I'm not sure what I want to do. I love my beautiful home in Lovely."

"Hire a manager and keep it to run as you planned," he told her pulling her toward the bedroom.

"What a great idea." Tesha beamed at him and then let out a peal of laughter when she didn't move fast enough and he picked her up and carried her the rest of the way. His mouth took hers and she forgot about anything other than the wonderful man who would be her husband.

Later that night Tesha slipped from the bed. After ensuring Adam slept soundly, she went through the living room to the open balcony.

Her robe flapped in the breeze as she took in the night sky. "David. I wanted to tell you that I am in love. I'm getting married again." She waited for a few beats and smiled. "You would like Adam. He's a good man. A brave man, who will make an amazing husband. I miss you, and know you are happy for me."

Adam came up behind her. He looked groggy and adorable with his hair all mused up. "Are you okay? It's like three o'clock in the morning."

Bare-chested, he wore only an old pair of sweatpants he must have pulled on when not finding her in the bed. Tesha's gaze traveled from his chiseled chest down the washboard stomach to the soft trail of hair. "You know…" she tapped her finger on his chin, "I am reminded of a day months ago when I knocked on your door and you opened it wearing those pants. I've wanted to explore that happy trail since the first day I saw you."

He scratched his head and yawned. "What trail?"

When her eyes locked to the spot just beneath his waistband, he looked down and both eyebrows lifted. "Oh."

She took his hands and walked backwards to the bedroom. "Yes. Oh."

Epilogue

THANK YOU FOR reading Even Heroes Cry. I thoroughly enjoyed writing this book and shed quite a few tears in the process. As a former soldier, who was lucky enough to serve during peacetime, I have a great admiration for those who have served during the war.

The next in the Fords of Nashville series will be a bit lighter, *The Last Hero*, is Jensen and Cassie's story.

Dear Reader,

I love hearing from my readers and am always excited when you join my newsletter to get a free book and to keep abreast of new releases and other things happening in my world. Newsletter sign up: https://goo.gl/jLzPTA.

USA Today Bestselling author Hildie McQueen pens captivating romances. The heroes are alpha males, the heroines are fiery, resilient women. You'll love the passionate romance and captivating action under a canopy of beautiful settings.

Her favorite past-times are traveling, reading and discovering tiny boutiques. She resides in a beautiful Georgia small-town with her super-hero husband Kurt, and three little dogs.

Website: www.HildieMcQueen.com
Facebook: facebook.com/HildieMcQueen
Email: Hildie@HildieMcQueen.com